Letters From the Ranch

By
Nancy Lee Tegart
And
Sharon Wass

Cover photo by Tracey Read.

Printed in Victoria, Canada.

Note for Librarians: a cataloguing record for this book that includes Dewey Classification and US Library of Congress numbers is available from the National Library of Canada. The complete cataloguing record can be obtained from the National Library□ online database at: www.nlc-bnc.ca/amicus/index-e.html

ISBN: 1-4120-1861-7

TRAFFORD

This book was published *on-demand* in cooperation with Trafford Publishing. On-demand publishing is a unique process and service of making a book available for retail sale to the public taking advantage of on-demand manufacturing and Internet marketing. **On-demand publishing** includes promotions, retail sales, manufacturing, order fulfilment, accounting and collecting royalties on behalf of the author.

Suite 6E, 2333 Government St., Victoria, B.C. V8T 4P4, CANADA
Phone 250-383-6864 Toll-free 1-888-232-4444 (Canada & US)
Fax 250-383-6804 E-mail sales@trafford.com
Web site www.trafford.com
TRAFFORD PUBLISHING IS A DIVISION OF TRAFFORD HOLDINGS, LTD.
Trafford Catalogue # 03-2239 www.trafford.com/robots/03-2239.html

10 9 8 7 6 5 4

I want to thank Reno Goodwin, Hubert Kirsch, Hap and Sharon Tegart, the Jim Tegart family, Tug Hansen, Tom Marr, George Deck, Guy Messerli, Dave Nixon, Bob and Pat McGaw, and Lil and Sibbolt Detmers for being there when I needed them on the Hidden Valley Ranch. I also want to thank the many wonderful people who continue to enable me to remain on the Corby Place Ranch that Lloyd and I always loved, especially my partner and nephew, Peter Tegart, who made me a part of his family so many years ago.

There are many people who deserve my thanks, but I feel that my somewhat mature memory may not remember you all. Please consider your mention in this book as my sincere thanks. I thank the Lord for granting me a long and rich life full of loving family and friends.

Nancy Lee Tegart

Thank you to all the wonderfully supportive people who have made this book a reality. Special thanks to my family for allowing me to spend so much time with Nancy and welcoming her into our home.

Sharon Wass

My Roots

Kennard

Father

Mother

I was born October 28, 1912 in Cirencester, Gloucestershire, England. When I was four my family moved to Birmingham, where my father had accepted a position as the French language master at King Edward's High for boys. Birmingham, located in the midlands, was then the second largest city in England. Our home was in a middle class area of attached houses. The long rows of attached houses had joint entries like a tunnel, where we wheeled our bikes into our respective gardens. The entries faced onto a paved road, where we hopped, skipped, played rounders, and of course got to know the neighborhood children.

Ours was a comfortable three story dwelling with an airy top floor that served as bedroom for my sister Mary and myself. The middle floor consisted of a large bedroom for my parents, a spare room, a bathroom, and a playroom. Many plays were put on in this playroom, mostly history, with chairs arranged for the audience. The main floor had a large front facing living room, a dining room, a kitchen, and a scullery that led out to a lovely back yard. My one clear memory of our arrival at the new house at 40 Esme Road, Sparkhill was walking into the bathroom and seeing a leafy branch from a fruit tree on the windowsill. I imagine it came from a neighbor's yard.

By 1917 we were a family of five: my father, Arnold Lee; my mother, Dorothy Eliza Lee (nee Heath); myself; my sister

Mary Josephine, born January 15, 1914; and my brother Arnold Kennard (Ken) born August 2, 1916. My father came from a well-known farming family in Crediton, Devon but had no desire to stay on the farm. He had won at least one scholarship at Crediton Grammar School, which was rare in those days, so he pursued an academic career.

While on vacation with students from the King Edwards School over Easter break in 1925, he suffered a severe attack of appendicitis and was operated on in the British Hospital in Paris. It was probably one of the first such operations in those days. I always believed that this might have eventually contributed to his early death.

My father's brother, Cecil Lee, stayed on the family farm, "Holwell". It was a 500-acre sheep farm two miles from Crediton in County Devon, which is one of the southernmost counties in England. It is in the southwest next to Cornwall. "Holwell" had many interesting meadows, which I dearly loved to explore. The farmhouse was a large thatch roofed house that had a larder with a dairy where a cool stream ran over flat stones. Large round dishes of milk were cooled in the stream to obtain the cream for which Devon is so famous. To my delight there were two huge shire horses that were used for all the farm work. Bankruptcy had been looming for "Holwell", but during WW1, when the demand for beef was high, the farm profited because Uncle Cecil had good skills in buying and feeding butcher stock and kept cattle as well as the usual 500 sheep.

I have wonderful fond memories of "Holwell" as we used to spend summers down at the farm. My sister Mary was never inclined to spend time outdoors. She would rather be inside reading. My Uncle used to convince her to go out by giving her a spoon with some salt on it tied to a long stick. He said if she sat quietly she would be able to lure a rabbit, and that she could keep any she caught. I did my bit coaxing Mary outdoors by telling her we could play with Uncle Cecil's two spaniels. Mary and I spent hours tearing around the farm, with the dogs harnessed and tied to sticks, pretending they were horses.

One of the biggest attractions for me was my uncle's horse, "Ginger". In the countryside, all transport was with horses. “Ginger” was a 16 hand chestnut hunter used in the dogcart for trips into Crediton for shopping etc. A dogcart is a high, two wheeled vehicle, which got its name because it was high enough for a dog to go under it. A great thrill for me was when Uncle Cecil would throw me up onto "Ginger’s" back, and slap his hindquarters to send us on a tour of the farm.

There was one particularly memorable trip into Crediton, with "Ginger" harnessed to the dogcart and mother at the reins. It was an uneventful trip going in, but coming back was exciting. "Ginger" had been stabled while we were shopping and having hair-dos done. At departure time he was harnessed up again. It took three stalwart men to hold him until we were safely aboard. When mother said, “Let him go”, he plunged into a canter through the village, across the ford with a great splash and up the hill, where he at last settled down to a steady trot along the narrow, high-hedged road.

My mother was the eldest girl in a family of six children. Her family owned G.H. Heath and Co. Silk Throwsters of Maccelsfield, Cheshire. Mother knew the meaning of money for while growing up her family was well off. However, life had not always been easy for the Heath family. My great-grandfather, Dr. Fredrick Heath was swindled by his solicitor, who took off to Australia with Fredrick’s life savings. My grandfather, George Henry Heath, the eldest son, began his work career as an office boy in the silk mill. He worked hard learning everything he could, and finally became owner of the mill.

In the first years of this century the silk for England came from Japan and was transported across Canada by train, then shipped to England. Timing was very important to the quality of the silk and all train traffic across Canada was side tracked to allow the “silk train” speedy crossing.[1]

---

[1] “Silk trains”, Columbo’s Canadian References, 1976 p. 485 “Crack CPR freight trains that crossed the continent from Vancouver to New York, between the First and Second World Wars, loaded with raw silk that came from Japan on the Empress Lines. They traveled at high speeds to deter possible hijackers and to lessen demurrage, so valuable was their cargo.”

There were only two locations in England where the climate was conducive to silk manufacturing and Maccelsfield was one of them. At G.H Heath and Co. the silk throwsters threw the silk from the cocoon onto the spool. The history of Maccelsfield is interwoven with the silk industry.

Relating to what happened to me before coming to Canada is strangely enough, fairly easy. Bicycles were the city mode of transport for business folk. I remember that my father rode his bicycle to school each day. He had a beautiful B.S.A. (Birmingham Small Arms) 3-speed bike, state of the art in those days. I wanted my own bike but I was told I was too young. One day when our parents were away, probably to a tennis tournament as dad had won a few cups, I dared to try and ride my father's big bike. They came home and found me circling in front of the house with my leg through the crossbar. Father decided then that it was best to get me my own bicycle and he found me a second hand one. I eventually got a nice new bike. We children were given six pence a week pocket money. A chart was kept on the wall and if we were careless and left our bicycles out in the rain we lost one penny.

It was my responsibility to look after the family dog. I had to feed it and walk it. The first one I remember is an Airedale. We always believed that he was stolen. Next came "Bobbie", a black and tan, smooth-haired Terrier. Mother was very strict about no dogs on the beds. She did allow me to make a bed out of chairs beside my bed for the dog to sleep on.

Mary and I were day pupils at Mosely College for girls on Showell Green Lane and we rode to school, about 2 miles, regardless of the weather. It was a strict school where we wore uniforms, white blouse, yellow and blue tie, navy tunic, and a felt hat with a yellow and blue band. I was a good student overall. I enjoyed spelling and so added my marks to the friendly competition between houses. The students were divided into houses. My house was St. Brides. Unfortunately I was no mathematician, and although I tried hard to learn my multiplication tables, I often stood in the corner, supposedly learning.

Poor behavior, on or off school, meant disgrace. If you were caught, you were not allowed to wear your hatband or tie, so the whole school knew you were in disgrace. I discovered this the hard way one day, when I played truant to try and catch tadpoles in a swamp on the way to school. The school reported that I was not there. There were unpleasant questions that had to be answered and for the next month I had no tie or hatband.

I enjoyed collecting pictures of horses, mostly hunting scenes. I rarely missed a Tom Mix and Tony matinee and I was an avid reader of all western stories. I also loved dogs, especially German Shepherds. I subscribed to Dog World magazine and kept up with the champions of Crofts, Britain's major dog show.

Tom Mix and Tony movies were not the only matinees I went to. I remember a series about a Chinese doctor who trained a gorilla to kill people he didn't like. In one show the gorilla was reaching into a hospital room to kill a man when the person guarding the man cut off the gorilla's arm with an axe. The gorilla, mad with pain went back and killed the Chinese doctor. I had nightmares after that and it was father who took me back to bed and sat with me until I slept.

We weren't a terribly close family. I remember many times when my father went to see his family, while mother took us to see hers, especially at Christmas time. My mother's parents had moved to the north Lake District when Grandfather Heath retired. I would like to have known my Devonshire family better. I also wish now, looking back, that it had been easier to spend more time with my cousins in Cheshire, Mother's brother Noah's family. They were great hunting folk, with gorgeous thoroughbred hunters. Uncle Noah was the master of the local hunt. I loved horses, even if my only practical knowledge was being thrown up on "Ginger" as he did his tour of Farm Holwell.

On Saturdays in the spring, if it were not raining, Mary, Ken, "Bobbie", and I would take a bus ride and follow the river that ran out of Birmingham into the country, looking for tadpoles. Don't ask me now what we wanted them for, or what we did with them. I have no idea.

One Saturday, April 2, 1923, I had caught a cold and was not allowed to go with Mary and Ken when they set out for the river. For some reason they left the river and went over to a football field that had a big pond with a raft in it. I suppose Mary and Ken went out on the raft trying to catch tadpoles. Ken must have slipped into the water, and Mary, being unable to swim couldn't save him. She called for help to some boys that were playing football, but Ken drowned.

I had been taking swimming lessons at the time and I have always believed that I might have saved him if I had been there. Even now I am filled with the deepest sorrow for what Mary must have gone through as she called the footballers for help. Mary never talked about it. Understandably I suppose. My mother must have been devastated as Ken was destined to be in the family firm of G.H. Heath & Co. My father must also have been upset by Ken's death as he lost his only son. A few years later, Uncle Cecil's only son also died young by slipping into the cider machine at the farm.

We weren't told much about Ken's death as we were really shielded from many things in those days. We knew very little about the mysteries of death or birth. Of course we weren't alone. Children in urban England lacked the advantage of farm animals to learn the facts of life and parents did not talk about them. My mother had always been a stout woman and knew how to dress well, so I never realized she was pregnant. When my sister Joan was born, March 13, 1925, I believed, as did many children at that time, that she came in the doctor's bag. One memory I have of the arrival of the new baby is that the bus driver on our route must have been as unaware of my mother's condition as I was, because he asked my mother whose baby she was.

As I said, children were shielded from all upsetting circumstances in those days. I only found out about the details of Ken's death long after he had died. Likewise, when father took ill, we children knew only to "please be quiet" as we passed his bedroom door. When he died, December 12, 1926, we were not told, but were sent to stay with relatives.[2] It was only in 2002 that I learned his death was caused from septic pneumonia and meningitis. These sad events were never

[2] Obituary in Appendix 1

discussed before children. I was only thirteen years old when he died. I wish I had had the opportunity to get to know my father better, as I know he was a fine man.

Sometime after father's death, at breakfast one morning, my mother asked us if we would like to go to Canada. What an unnecessary question. I was ecstatic. My dream of living in the Wild West was coming true. Mary, fifteen months younger, couldn't care less what we did. She had always been sickly and subject to serious bouts of whooping cough. Mary was usually in the house reading, while I loved being outside skipping or playing rounders. Because of Mary's health, the doctor had ordered a change in climate. Since Mother's income would go much farther living in Canada than in England, she accepted her sister Barbara's invitation to come live with them.

Barbara, mother's younger sister, had married Eric Smith, who was from a Somerset brewing family. Eric's mother and sister had both died of consumption and Eric tended to have a weak chest as well. Eric had come to Canada with a friend in 1908 and spent the summer in southern Alberta. Memories of how healthy he had felt that summer made Eric wish to return to Canada.

In 1913 Barbara and Eric were married and shortly after their first son, Geoff, was born in 1914, they moved to Canada. They stayed two years north of Edgewater, British Columbia at what is now called Spur Valley. Ted was born May 1916 and shortly after that they went to the Dominion Experimental Farm in Invermere, where the Invermere District Hospital is today. Spring of 1918 Dorothy was born and in September they purchased the U5 Ranch near Edgewater. After my father died Barbara wrote and invited mother to come stay with them awhile.

Moves did not occur overnight in those days, so it was the better part of a year before we were ready to leave for Canada. Aunt Barbara had come over to help mother with the arrangements and be our guide. During this time precious things of my father's were sold. I remember a metal gondola on a revolving bookcase from our living room that had been a souvenir of my father's travels in Venice. All his gold engraved, leather-bound books went. I did not miss these items until many years later, but of course children were not consulted in any decisions.

One of the few things that really upset me was that I had to give away my new bicycle. I had worked hard at being responsible for a long time before my father let me have that bicycle. I also regretted leaving our dog "Bobbie". Our last few weeks in England were spent at the Careless Farm near Warwick. It was a happy time for me. I spent as much time as I could at the stables. We left "Bobbie" with our friends at the Careless farm.

Father's family home, "Holwell Barton Farm", at Crediton, Devon.

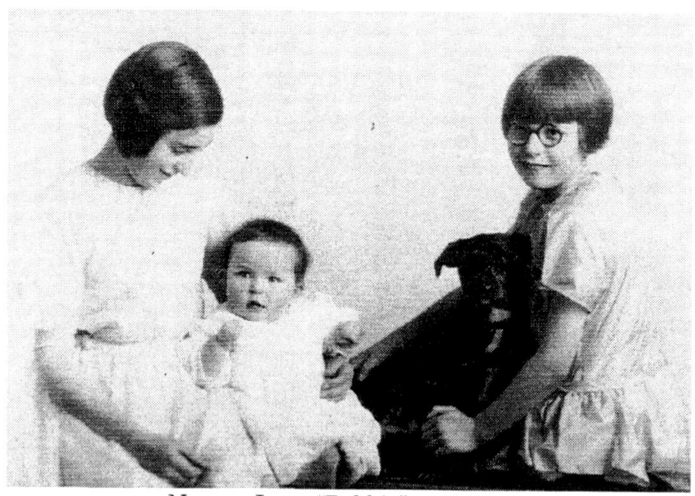

Nancy, Joan, "Bobbie", and Mary

Life at the U5 Ranch

The cousins at the U5 Ranch, 1928. Back - Geoff Smith and Nancy Lee.
Front - Charles Smith, Dorothy Smith, Joan Lee, Mary Lee and Ted Smith.

I remember little of the weeklong voyage by ship from Liverpool, England to Quebec, Canada. During the passage none of us were seasick. After we landed though, my two-year-old sister, Joan, in her high chair at the hotel in Quebec had what was called land sickness. Safe and sound on dry land she belatedly developed stomach upset.

On the CPR train across Canada to Golden, my only thought was, "What will Golden look like?" When we arrived, all I could see that appeared "golden" were masses of dandelions. Uncle Eric Smith met us in John Blakley's large Dodge touring car, which was seldom used, as the roads were not conducive to automobile traffic in those days. Uncle sometimes used this car in the summer to take meat, milk and vegetables up to Radium for tourists at the parking lot above the pool. More often horses were used.

It was May, 1927 when we arrived in Golden. I do not remember the journey to Edgewater and the U-5 Ranch, but I remember the feeling of actually being on a real ranch. I was in seventh heaven. Aunt Barbara's children, Geoffrey, Dorothy, Ted, and Charles, waited at the ranch to greet the new arrivals from England. With three new cousins and the three adults, there were eleven at the supper table. The next year my cousin Meg was born.

My Uncle Eric's brother, Archie, lived just across the hayfield. I remember that he had a government contract for grading the roads with a team of horses each summer. I remember Uncle Archie's wedding. It was my first country wedding and I really enjoyed it.

The U-5 Ranch is a beautiful piece of property located between Edgewater and Radium Hot Springs. For those unfamiliar to the geography it is located in the Columbia River Valley of British Columbia with the Rocky Mountains raising majestically to the east and the mighty Purcell range on the west. It is a lovely, wide valley and the Columbia River, only 70 km from its source, is a wide slow moving river with luscious slough land surrounding it. The U-5 ranch land spreads down to the river and straddles the road. Looking west from the Ranch yard you can see the prow of Steamboat Mountain. It is the first thing to catch the sun in the morning and a shadowy giant by evening. To this city girl fresh from England, it all seemed like paradise.

The main road between Golden and Invermere was gravelled and ran between the ranch hay fields. Clouds of dust heralded car traffic and my boy cousins always knew who it was. Not me, but as time went by, I knew people by their horses. The ranch was the stopping place for many folk, such as ranchers, guides, and outfitters with livestock, frequently going from Windermere to Brisco, some of whom would stay overnight. There was great excitement as they drove their stock to the corrals. That is where I first saw my dream horse "Rainbow". He was owned by the Tegart family and usually ridden by Buster Tegart. "Rainbow" was a beautiful showy part hackney gelding. The boys enjoyed showing off with him to a green English teenager. He thrilled me. I promised myself to someday own a chestnut "Rainbow".

Practically all transportation in the Columbia Valley in 1927, especially during the winter, was with horses. There were no government snowploughs in those days. In the winter there were many bobsleigh trips to Edgewater for church, dances, weddings, etc. Box socials were a new experience for Mary and me. The men did not know who had made the boxes and vied to find out before the bidding. I had my first taste of alcohol at one dance. Once in awhile we would go all the way to Brisco for a dance in Henry Duhammel's car. We made a stop in Edgewater at Leonard Geddes' house and I had my first drink.

The bobsleighs were large with wide runners and were used for heavy farm or logging work. When used for a trip to town, the large wagon box was filled with hay, hot bricks, foot warmers, and blankets. Blankets were especially important for the horses who were always heated and had to stand in the cold while we were inside, enjoying ourselves. There was no need to urge the team on the way home!

My cousin, Dorothy Brown, recently reminded me of another memory from the U-5 days. It was in the summer of 1927, our first summer here. Mother, fresh from England, always insisted we dress for supper. A pink cotton dress had recently arrived from Eaton's, our only source for shopping, and mother insisted I wear it for supper. After supper, Uncle Eric asked my oldest cousin, Geoff, to go out and look for a cow that he was expecting to calve. Uncle didn't give a thought to the yearling registered Ayrshire bull that was down in the pasture. I wanted to go along, so we set out to look for the missing cow. It was a rough pasture, approximately 1000 acres that went from the buildings down to the river. There were other cattle in the pasture, but we continued to look for the cow we had been sent to find. I was unaware of the yearling Ayrshire bull, which must have taken offence at my dress. He charged and knocked me to the ground. I dread to think what would have happened if Geoff had not been there and hit him on the nose with a stick. The bull disappeared! The dress was torn right across the middle and was quite unwearable. I was secretly quite pleased that I would not have to wear it again.

There were many horses on the U5 to get to know and love during those early days in Canada. I got to know some much better than others, but I was in heaven getting to know them all. I also got to know several of the neighbours' horses as well, particularly the Tegart's as they often stopped by.

"Lady" was a dear, old, sway-backed mare that I would ride to school if Ted were not driving us. The school was a one room log building built by my uncle beside the McCauley Creek. Prior to it being built, Emily Tegart had taught my cousins at the ranch. "Lady" was so gentle that if her saddle slipped under her tummy, she would just stop and wait for you to cinch properly.

"Ben" was a fine, dependable worker on the U5. He was probably 14 - 1600 lbs., and although you could not deny he was chubby, he was very athletic and could jump a gate standing beside it.

"Black Bess," 1800 lb., part Percheron and her partner "Smokey" 1900 lb., part Clydesdale, worked on the road. The Big Bend highway construction between Golden and Revelstoke helped many farmers and ranchers with their taxes and other expenses through the Depression. If a team could be spared from the farm, that is where they went for the summer. "Black Bess" and "Smokey" were also used for logging in the winter.

"White Nellie" was a grey mare and mother to "Pete" and "Dick." She was used for many things, but mainly for the buggy to take Aunt Barbara to Edgewater for mail, groceries, and church. "Nellie" was often used with "Dick" as a team for raking hay and for the democrat, a larger version of the buggy, which held several passengers

"Pete" was pig eyed, raw-boned, jug headed, and not dependable. I never knew who had started halter breaking "Pete," but Ted and I were told to use him one day. He broke every halter and rope, so we decided to use a logging chain. Our one mistake was using it on a tree on the main road opposite the house. There was "Pete" sitting down doing his best to break that chain. There were roars of protest at such cruelty. If left alone, I feel sure he would have learned his lesson. The result was he was never used.

"Dick" was a grey, well-built gelding about 14 hands high. He was Ted's special joy and often took us to school in the buggy or the cutter, depending on the season. Ted did the driving, and a trick Ted used to love playing on us was driving "Dick" up on a snow bank and tipping us out. We had only one choice, walk the two miles to school. When Ted rode "Dick", he liked to show off by asking "Dick" to rear up. This made a pretty picture as "Dick" had a short thick neck.

In the 20's and 30's, Alex Ritchie was the Valley auctioneer and general livestock provider, whose home was located at what is now Wilfley's Swansea Rock Ranch. If one needed a cow or a horse, Alex was the man. Uncle bought a nice part-Clydesdale mare named "Nellie." She had to be renamed "Black Nellie" to distinguish her from Aunt Barbara's "White Nellie." She became a favourite of mine.

Tretheway's had a big team of bald-faced Clydesdales that bought the threshing machine every fall to the U-5 and other ranches. Those were busy days, hauling the sheaves in the big hayracks from the fields. The women were kept busy cooking huge meals for the hungry folk. At the end of threshing we had to pull the machine up the hill to the road. This needed an extra team and Ted and I vied with each other as to who would drive the team.

As my only practical knowledge of horses, prior to arriving at the U-5, was on Uncle Cecil's horse "Ginger," I needed a lot of guidance the first few weeks. My cousin, Ted, and ranch hand, Bill Harrison, who worked for my Uncle, encouraged and helped me a lot. Ted, three years younger than I, was born and raised to ranch life. He knew horses and enjoyed the opportunity to initiate his "green" cousin to the horses. Ted and I became best buddies. Many were the scrapes the two of us got into. Ted was a natural ventriloquist and could imitate a coyote's howl or a mare's whinny. He often scared my sister, Joan, at bedtime by making a coyote howl under the veranda.

I was riding "Dick" one day on the road just outside the ranch house, trying to get a bull into the yard. The bull refused and proceeded to push "Dick" over the fence. Happily, it was a wooden fence, not high, protecting two Larmour graves, and no harm was done. I learned driving a bull is a different critter to a cow. You need a good dog!

An exciting event that Ted and I always enjoyed was taking cattle for market to the Firlands corral at the Radium Kootenay Central Stockyards, near the present airstrip by the mill. As I have said, the country was wide open then, no fences. The cattle in strange country were often difficult to handle, but I believe we always succeeded in corralling them safely at Firlands

We did a lot of work with horses: driving teams especially in haying time, hauling loose hay from the field, raking hay into windrows ready for cocking, with the use of a pitchfork, which was an everyday tool. The hay rake used a team, usually "Nellie" and "Dick". You had to know what you were doing when pitching hay onto the load. A badly built load of loose hay could often be a disaster when crossing irrigation ditches en route to the barn. One good horse or a team was needed for the hayfork, which took the hay from the wagon up into the loft, where the fork was tripped before returning for another load from the wagon. Two hayfork loads usually emptied the wagon.

I remember one occasion during haying at the U-5; I was driving a team with a large hayrack, which had been left overnight by the hay barn. The team wasn't "Nellie" and "Dick," it was "Bill" and his partner. "Bill" was never reliable. He was a large angular horse with an ugly head, mean little eyes, and huge ears. While hitching up, as I was behind the team hooking up the heel chains, something upset old "Bill" and he bolted. I was caught between the team and the wagon as the team took off. The rack was only feet from the corner of the barn. The rack caught the corner of the barn, which lifted the rack off its wheels and over a sharp drop in the bank that was cribbed with logs. I was thrown off my feet, caught between horses and wagon. In desperation, I clung to the pole and was dragged under the wagon as the team went around the barn and was finally stopped in the yard on the north side of the barn.

Ted and I did get into mischief in our spare time. The whole country was wide open with no fences, except the ranch's hayfields. There were scores of domestic horses that had gone wild in the countryside. They had thousands of acres of range to roam freely. At night, the wild horses would use the main road between the two large hay fields to get from one range to another.

One evening we lay in wait, Ted to whinny like a mare, me to put up the bars. Ted's whinny lured the stallion into the well-built, high, log corral in the fence along the road and I quickly threw up the bars. When the stallion was in the corral Ted tried to rope him, but he jumped out of the corral into the huge wild pasture that ran down to the river.

We didn't say a word to anyone, but every night we tried to snare that stallion, making a loop over trees on the trail that he ran along. Finally we did lasso him but again he got away, this time trailing a good lariat into a newly seeded, freshly irrigated field with water running in carefully guided ditches about two feet apart. The stallion ploughed straight across this field, hock deep in mud, and gained firm ground before hitting the barbed wire fence, where he knocked down several posts and escaped with that expensive lariat. This escapade cost Ted and me many hours of hard work after school for some time. That lariat could eventually have cost the stallion his life if it had become entangled on a tree or bush. I often wondered what happened to the lariat and who paid for it, it was probably Bill Harrison's.

Bill was very knowledgeable about horses and livestock and he seemed to enjoy helping me to learn my way around horses. I, a very green English girl, didn't properly appreciate the luxury of having someone ride ahead and hold branches out of my way and other courtesies Bill showed me. On trail rides looking for cattle, we were often up at the Ward Ranch, a pretty spot southeast of the U-5, now or recently part of the Upper Ranch, Statham's summer pasture for cattle.

My first year at the ranch a little roan pony, I believe belonging to the Geddes', was an eye-opener for me. When Bill and I were out looking for cattle, he would smell every bush on the trail. He knew what we were looking for. Some time after our arrival in Canada an unfortunate comment Bill made in Invermere, about wanting to marry me when I grew up, got back to my mother and Bill was let go. I was too young to know about this. It wasn't until years later I found out the real reason for Bill's dismissal.

When Bill left the ranch in 1928, I was allowed to leave school at the age of 15 and was put temporarily in charge of the horse barn. The Depression was on us, and though I was kept home, Mary and Geoff were sent to high school in Salmon Arm. A friend of my Uncle's, Jack Allen, who built the one and only hotel in Edgewater, boarded Geoff and Mary while they were at school.

Back in the Depression and post-war years, the Valley had plenty of snow in the winters and the horses were all sharp shod, sometimes with disastrous results. John McCollough from Sinclair Creek near Radium was the postmaster for Radium. John went to Firlands, the Railway station for Radium, to meet the train in the cutter or buggy, winter and summer. John had a cantankerous, blue roan horse called "Old Blue," who was pretty handy with his hind feet. John came to the ranch for a visit and "Old Blue" was turned out into the corral with dear old "Lady," who would not hurt a flea. Later, "Lady" was found with a very deep cut in her chest. It lay open and you could put your hand in it. I was told to throw lime in it every day (lime was always kept for the outdoor biffies). I was amazed when the cut healed beautifully with no scar.

"Pigeon" was the first horse I owned. Buster, and Jim Tegart often stopped in with livestock at the U5 Ranch, en route to either the Alpine Ranch at Windermere or to the Tegart property (the Igloo) in Brisco. Buster told mother he would find a horse for me. Mother had said any horse for me must have "blood" in it. This greatly amused Buster apparently, but he knew what mother meant. As a girl in London, she had been given instructions on tandem driving, one horse ahead of the other, so she knew good horses.

In those days, any unbranded horse over a year old that was loose on the range was up for grabs. Buster arrived with a thin two-year-old, green broke, half-thoroughbred gelding that he had caught on the range unbranded. He was black with a white star and stood about 15 hands. Mother paid him $50, a good sum then.

The horse was thin, so Ted and I put him down in the big 1,000-acre pasture below the ranch buildings and stole a feed of oats to him every night. When we finally decided it was time to ride him, he had forgotten what little he knew. Good thing I was young and my bones did not break easily. Ted would hold him while I climbed on. "Pigeon" lit into bucking. I did not realize then that he was bucking! I couldn't count how many times he piled me. I just kept climbing on until he finally gave up. "Pigeon" carried me well for many years.

Eventually my uncle hired new hands, cousins Llew and Trevor Jones, who were fresh from Wales. In those days, new immigrants were required to work on a farm for a year before they could apply for permanent citizenship. One morning in the barn, I found poor "White Nellie" at the end of her halter rope, sitting like a dog trying to avoid Llew who was endeavouring to put her collar on the English way! At that time in England, horses' collars were fitted and stayed with the horse all its life. Turned upside down, it went over the horse's head and then was turned around. (Probably all English harness horses still wear unopened collars, or breast collars.) Canadian collars open at the top. I said, "Llew, that is not how you do it," and took the collar and showed him how it worked.

"Black Nellie" was a dependable, willing, workhorse, except when in heat. Then she would try and kick her team mate over the pole. In the summer of 1928, Trevor and I had quite an experience during haying time. We were walking the horses to the hay wagon and the grass was slippery. I had tried to change "Nellie" from her usual position to the left side. She did not like that and tried to take the bit in her teeth and run. I lost my footing and fell, but refused to let go of the lines. Trevor leapt to help me and there we were rolling and sliding hanging onto the lines. Our combined weight finally stopped the team and I put "Lady" back on the right.

Later Trevor and Llew left Radium for Ottawa in an ancient car with wooden wheels. Llew became an R.C.M.P. officer, and Trevor became principal of Guelph Veterinary College in Guelph, Ontario. Trevor celebrated his 90th birthday in Victoria in July 1999. I couldn't resist reminding him of this incident in my birthday telegram to him. It is in his book *Trevor's Story.*

Uncle often had new immigrants working on the ranch. They all were quite particular about dressing for supper and having shined shoes, just as my mother had been. I remember one family, the Halls, who would sit out on the steps of the ranch house polishing their shoes every morning. Mr. Hall went on after the ranch to work at the Kootenay Park Gate for a while. One time a tourist asked where the restroom was and an embarrassed Mr. Hall had to admit that he didn't know what they were talking about. "Restroom" was a Canadian term he was unfamiliar with. We had a good laugh around the dinner table when he shared the story.

Shortly after we moved to the ranch mother helped the Smiths add on three rooms to make room for us all. Usually only family stayed in the house, as there was a bunkhouse for the temporary help. Of course some people stayed in the house, but I remember Aunt Barbara being quite adamant about "No strangers in the house".

In 1928 there was a bumper hay crop and Uncle Eric needed a few extra hands. It was the start of the great depression and many men were walking the roads looking for work. They usually packed their own bedrolls and would work for a day or a week, however long you could hire them. Two men showed up right in time for haying, but there was no room in the bunkhouse. Uncle Eric really needed the help so he convinced Aunt Barbara to let them stay in the house. We took to referring to the new hands as Mutt and Jeff due to their physical similarities to the cartoon characters. Some time after they left there was an infestation of bed bugs, which resulted in each room needing to be sealed off and sulphur candles burnt to exterminate the pests. I am sure that Uncle Eric was reminded of it for a very long time.

Radium Hot Springs

Bob Tegart taking the Richter's home over the Settler's Road

Just south of the U-5, the Kootenay Park Highway had only been open for a few years. There was nothing but Bill Morpeth's trappers cabin at the present town site of Radium. The settlement, such as it was, was located where the Radium Hot Springs Pools are today. There was the RCMP detachment and stable, the park gate with Sandy Gordon's house and garage, the CPR cabins (which are now at Fairmont), the pool, of course, and John and Jessie Blakley's hotel, garage and store. There were no banks as yet in Radium, and Dunn and Bradstreet, a large credit company, was the only source for credit. My uncle, Eric Smith, was the local Dun and Bradstreet representative. Uncle Eric also wintered National Park horses and delivered supplies and firewood to the Blakley's Hotel. During the time I was at the ranch, I was usually the deliverer.

The road from the U-5 Ranch where we lived at the time, to Blakley's Hotel in Radium, turned down into Sinclair Creek where Deck's campground is now, then up the hill toward Radium. It was a steep climb both ways for the horses. I recall one trip in the spring of 1928; "White Nellie" and "Dick" were hitched to the democrat, and Aunt Barbara and I were taking the usual milk and vegetables to Blakley's Hotel in Radium. At that time of the year, with the frost coming out and the steep overhang of the Sinclair Canyon, falling rock was a common occurrence. When we reached the canyon, I stopped the team and told Auntie that I was running them through the canyon. I knew that if a rock fell on them while walking, they would be startled, whereas if I urged them to run (which no well-trained horse would be allowed to do), they would think it was me. Auntie said very primly, "I will walk through." Which she did, keeping well under the towering cliff.

I remember another trip to Blakley's Hotel with "Dick," who was always a mischievous horse. "Dick" was hitched to the cutter and tied at the Blakley's Hotel while I was having lunch with Ed Orr. Ed was an elderly man with a limp who was the gatekeeper for the Kootenay National Park. He also used to cut hair for the local folk. Ed was going to cut my hair at the gate, which was about a hundred yards from the hotel. I wanted to take "Dick" with us, but Ed, a knowledgeable horseman, said, "Oh, he's all right." So I gave in, much to my ultimate sorrow.

Ed had apparently forgotten all about "Jock", a beautiful, black, part-thoroughbred horse that belonged to the RCMP. Constable Summerfield was in charge at Radium, where "Jock" was stabled beside his home (on the ground where Radium Lodge now stands). The RCMP, like everyone else, depended on horses for much of their transportation. Every day, it was the custom to let "Jock" loose to go down to the creek for water. In doing so, the trail went down beside the hotel. I was watching while perched on a high stool in Ed's office and saw "Jock" prance up to "Dick" to play. I was recently informed that eight-year old Herb Blakley tried to stop Jock, only to have Jock turn on him.

"Jock" started nibbling poor "Dick" who finally reared up, broke his halter rope and took off out of sight with the cutter swishing from side to side. I tore out of the office, hair half cut, with poor, lame Ed hobbling behind me. All I saw when I reached the corner opposite the hotel, was milk bottles all over the road. Looking anxiously for the horses, I saw them standing quietly, "Dick's" blanket half on, half off, under some trees up the bank. The cutter was on a stump, harness in shreds. I was in shock thinking I would never be allowed to drive again. Ed consoled me as he pulled the cutter off the stump, "Don't worry, we will fix things up."

"Dick" came quietly down to the road and we got the cutter back to the Gordon's garage beside the gate. Luckily the garage was large enough for both the cutter and the horse. Ed finished cutting my hair and got me a cup of tea. I think it must have been Mrs. Gordon, Peggy Statham's mother, who gave me the tea while Ed mended the harness with the ever-useful haywire. When he led "Dick" out for me to go home, he gave him a good jerk on the bit to remind him to behave. Not a word was said at the ranch. Ed must have phoned.

In July of 2000, I was talking to Ward Wilder, nee Gordon, and she was telling me about her memories of "Jock" from her childhood in Radium. She said she remembers her mother saying that "Jock" was so full of beans and high spirits from being well-fed and underworked, that when hitched to the cutter coming round the corner by the hotel, he'd come so fast the cutter would tip over. History does not relate what happened to the driver. Life at that time was full of accidents with horses.

Another memory I have of "Jock" is the beautiful picture he made when RCMP Constable Summerfield and his wife, Daphne, would come to visit my Uncle and Aunt at the U-5 in winter. "Jock" was a beautiful black gelding and as he had a red harness with bells, when they came to visit on a clear winter day, with a red lined fur robe over their knees, they made a lovely picture.

Riding up to the Radium Hot Springs for a dip was not done often from the U-5 ranch, but when we did, we always rode "over the top" as we called it. We went up the north side of Sinclair Canyon coming down to the road just below the Blakley's garage and store, where Blakley's Bungalow's stood up until 2002. As you can imagine, it saved a long ride down into the Sinclair Creek and up the hill again to where Radium town site is now.

One evening when I was still learning to ride Johnny Blakley stopped in. He asked Uncle Eric, "Did you know you had an acrobat in your family?" He was looking right at me! "Nancy was bringing in the cows," he continued. "Down in the lower pasture, she put the horse at a log and went from its shoulders to its tail and didn't come off." I had been riding bareback, as Uncle said, “No saddle for six months”. Needless to say, there were hoots of laughter from everyone except me.

Another time Johnny stopped in at suppertime to tell us about a shooting in Radium. The game warden had stopped in to Bill Morpeth’s cabin to warn him to be careful with his grass burning and not let it spread. Old Bill must have been offended by the comment and shot and killed the warden. I was still a green English girl with visions of Tom Mix and Tony style frontier battles. After all the usual comments in reaction to a tragedy I innocently said, "I thought this happened all the time." More hoots of laughter.

In 1928, the Kootenay National Park road was only open for vehicles in the summer. Much work had yet to be done widening and gravelling what was literally only a dirt road, not wide enough in many places for two to pass. This project provided much needed work for valley residents for a few years. Many horses, ploughs and slips were used. A slip was similar in size to a large wheelbarrow. The slip had no wheels, but lay on the ground and was pulled by one or two horses. When you lifted the handles, the metal lip dug into the ground filling the slip with dirt. With handles down, the slip was taken to where the contents were needed, the handles were raised and the slip was emptied. There was a larger, similar machine, drawn I think by four or more horses. I believe it was called a fresno. Where the brushed out road was wide enough, the fresno was used.

The park horses, mostly with some draft blood, were wintered at the U5 Ranch at Edgewater, as Uncle Eric had a contract with Kootenay Park. There were several teams and the park wardens’ pack and saddle horses. When the Kootenay Park road camps closed for the winter these horses spent a happy few weeks on the hayfields at the ranch before they were moved to the river sloughs where they would stay until March, or whenever the river opened. My cousin Ted and I usually had a heated discussion as to who got to take them to the sloughs where they would remain until early spring. Of course, Uncle Eric had the final say, but Ted and I enjoyed the competition.

“Shorty” was one of the heavy workhorses from the road crew. He was part Clydesdale, an excellent worker, but a poor keeper. He would not have fared well on the sloughs, so he and his teammate were kept in the barn and did winter work for the ranch. One of "Shorty's" chores, hauling firewood, often became my task to drive. There was one very memorable trip to Blakley's Hotel with "Shorty" and his teammate.

It was a gorgeous sunny day, with plenty of snow (plenty of snow was normal in those days). We were headed to Radium with a large sleigh load of firewood for Blakley's Hotel. It was a steep pull up from the spectacular Sinclair Canyon. Halfway up the hill, I turned the team sideways for a breather. As we rested, I was enjoying the scenery with the snow sparkling in the sun when two magnificent Rocky Mountain Bighorn rams jumped down from the bank. The horses pricked up their ears and I watched with amazement. The rams majestically walked away from each other until they were about fifty yards apart. They turned at exactly the same moment, went up on their hind legs, trotted toward each other, and came together with a very loud bang as their horns locked. Then they sedately walked away from each other and repeated the manoeuvre. I will never forget the sight.

Gypsy Years

1929 Saddle Club, L-R Jim Champion, Helen Young, Phyllis Young, Mary Lee, Roger Ruck and Nancy Lee

We had been in Canada two years when mother decided to move to Athalmer, an old municipality from steamship days on the Columbia River. I am sure that part of the reason was the simple fact that two women, Mother and Aunt Barbara, in one kitchen is one woman too many. There were eight children altogether. To my delight I had not spent a lot of time in the house as I was in charge of the horse barn; I did, however, have the chore of preparing lunches for the other children during the school year. Ever since then I have not liked sandwiches!

Mother rented a big old house in Athalmer that belonged to Frank Richardson, where the Esso Redi-Mart stands now. Frank was an old timer with quite a bit of property in the area. He also owned several head of Clydesdale horses, which ran loose on the sloughs and uplands where the Shuswap Indian Reserve is now. Athalmer was mainly swamp and my horse "Pigeon" ran loose on the swamp to graze. During our stay in Athalmer, mother worked as a cook for the Invermere Hospital. Young Dave Nixon used to come in with the wood every morning and light the fires at the hospital. Many years later I became friends with his war bride, Ruby.

We all missed my father and one of the reasons was that he had been the firm parent. Mother was not nearly firm enough with Joan. One evening in Athalmer Joan was being very naughty and had run upstairs in a tantrum. From downstairs we heard a tremendous crash and we knew that it had to be mother's precious things from on top of her dresser. Mother turned to me and said, "Nancy, I can't handle this. You'll have to do so something about it."

Joan, who was 5 or 6 at the time, had run upstairs and pulled the dresser scarf and now all of mother's treasures lay on the floor. Joan was on the bed face down, kicking and screaming, in an excellent position for a spank. So that is what she got. I told her that she had better clean up the mess and come down and apologize to Mother. I returned downstairs and a bit later Joan crept down, slipped through the partially opened door, and going to mother, apologized contritely.

The Kootenay Railway train ran through Athalmer and stopped once a week on its way to Cranbrook. Men were riding the rods looking for work, and they got off the train making fires in the bush near the tracks. Most weeks at least one man stopped by our house and asked for a meal. These men had a mark on posts for where they could get a meal. Mother always said they could have a meal if they chopped some wood. There was an old livery stable two houses away where I used to store my gear and give "Pigeon" a feed of oats nightly. One fall a man who had taken a meal with us stole my chaps, probably because riding the rods was very cold. He was likely unaware that they belonged to me, as they were kept two houses away. I reported the loss to Bob Pritchard, the local constable.

About two months later Bob called on us and reported that my chaps had turned up in Winnipeg. The chaps and the man were brought back to the courthouse in Wilmer so he could face the theft charge. The only court at that time was in Wilmer, which is 2 miles north of Athalmer. After my mother didn't press charges, the court decided to place the man in jail for the winter where he would at least be warm and fed. I was glad to get my chaps back.

I had been allowed to leave school while at the ranch and it did not occur to me to pressure mother into letting me go back. Mary went to school in Invermere. There was no overpass back then, so you went up to Invermere via the winding road off the present day industrial park. I was enjoying a life of riding and hanging around with companions like Helen Annis, Phyllis Falconer, Thelma Bartle, Fern Nickleson, Jim Champion, Roger Ruck, and others. We formed the Windermere Saddle Club and went on many a merry ride and camping trip.

I took great pleasure in going down to the river on a hot day and riding across with "Pigeon". A good friend I made while we were living in Athalmer was Thelma Rauch, later Carlson. She and I went horse hunting for a holiday. I have a picture of "Pigeon" and me with Thelma on my dresser today.

"Pigeon" and I helped a friend build a corral up on the old Birny Place to catch a beautiful bay stallion. He caught the horse one day and green broke him enough to ride against me in the fall fair. The bay was on the inside and we were neck and neck. Billy's stallion wouldn't answer the bit and turned into the bush taking "Pigeon" and me with him

I got interested in agriculture by raising pigs, and became a member of the Junior Swine Club. The swine club was a forerunner of today's 4-H. I had some pigs, which I kept at our place in Athalmer until someone reported me for having pigs in the municipal limits. This was really a bit foolish as by this time Athalmer was no longer the main town and there were only a few residents. The main town was now up the hill in Invermere. Anyway, when Jim from the Creamery heard about this he offered to let me build a corral beside the creamery, a good ½ mile away, where they could be fed buttermilk. Two friends and I built the corral and I took the pigs over in gunnysacks and let them loose in the corral. Later that night I heard an oinking at the door. The pigs had dug under the corral and come home. We repaired the corral and there were no further escapes.

Our club was keen to learn more about all livestock. I was teamed up with Winston Wolfenden of Brisco to compete for the East Kootenay Livestock Judging. We were to judge horses, cattle, sheep, and pigs. The contest was held at McCrindle's Dairy Farm in Cranbrook in 1931. Winston and I won the McPherson Cup, first place for the East Kootenay. This opened the way to compete at the Coast, at government expense, for the provincial honours. If we had won we would have been taken to compete at the Royal Winter Fair in Toronto. It was written up in the Cranbrook Courier, and possibly the Wilmer Outcrop.

For reasons I have never known, or had an answer for, Winston could not accompany me to the Coast. This was a golden opportunity in those depression days. Needless to say I was very disappointed. I had to have a teammate in order to go. Ruth Peters, daughter of a local dairy farmer, volunteered to go with me. Unfortunately she hardly knew one end of a cow from the other. We traveled to Colony Farm in Essondale. The farm was connected to the mental institute at that time. To be brief, I won the Hon. H.H. Steven's bronze medal for highest marks as an individual judge in the province, but we did not go on to Toronto.

Around 1929-1930, the Tegarts, Bob, Buster, and Jim, were hunting horses in the Height of Land area north of Wilmer and I rode with them. Louis Robideau and Blake Palmer often rode with us as well. Wild horses were everywhere and as it was almost totally open range with no fences any domestic horses would join them given the opportunity. They were extremely hard to catch, as they knew the ways of men. My, those wild cayuses were smart. They would run down a well-used trail and double back in the trees and watch us thundering by. These horses, when we finally got them corralled, were sold to the government for fox feed at $5.00 a head. I can't remember how these cayuses were taken to Athalmer to the stock corral for shipping, but I have a photo of one shipment. Later, because the ranchers wanted them off the range, they were often shot. There was a bounty of $5.00 for a pair of ears. It was years later before the ranchers realized it was a mistake because the cayuses had kept the forest from spreading by nipping off the young trees in the spring.

While in Athalmer mother became friendly with Lloyd Tegart, who owned the Windermere Garage and gas station. In 1931 we moved to Windermere and rented one of Lloyd's houses on the old Auchinbach acreage opposite where the Windermere Community Hall is now. Quite often, when the garage was very busy in the summer, I would assist at the pumps. Lloyd was married to a woman named Gertrude. They had had a daughter, Doreen, who died in 1923. They had twins, Ken and Pat, who were 4 or 5 at the time we were living in Windermere. They also had two daughters, Dorothy and Joan.

My mother often helped in Lloyd and Gertrude's house and she told me about one time in February when Henry Duhamel, who worked in the garage, took the three ton truck up to the Olde Corby Place to get wood, taking Ken and Pat with him. They had a flat tire and there was no spare. Henry had no choice but to walk out for help. He told the twins to stay put in the truck, but when he returned they were gone. It was hours later, after many people had been combing the area for the children, that Lloyd found them. He had a vision of them going up hill, and sure enough that is where he found them.

That winter we cared for the Whitehouse Hotel while the owners, Mr. and Mrs. Rufus Kimpton of Windermere's Stolen Church fame, were away. I, of course, did the outside work. Miss Sheara, the housekeeper, would make me breakfast of porridge after I came in from tending the stock each morning. One time I said that I was getting tired of it, so Miss Sheara fixed that. The next morning, to my surprise and delight, I had Grapenuts on my porridge.

That winter Ed Tegart died on the sloughs where he had been trapping. Ed was the brother of Arthur Tegart. Arthur was the father of Lloyd and my riding friends Buster, Jim and Bob. Since the roads were closed due to deep snow Lloyd hired me and my team to go to the railway station in Athalmer to pick up his Aunt Mitchell, from Brisco, and the coffin that had come down from Golden. There were deep drifts on the road, particularly where the dip on Swansea Road is today. The horses had to plunge several times to get through. But get through we did, so Ed was given a proper funeral.

Bob Tegart was a real horse loving man and had some well-bred horses. He liked some of the range horses because they were tough cayuses and he always kept the best of the wild ones. "Rod" and "Rowdy," two of the wild ones, made an unprecedented trip in -48° F weather and 2-3 feet of snow in to Settlers Road to bring out sick Mrs. Frank Richter, after Frank had snow shoed over the Tegart Pass to the Alpine Ranch for help. Alfred Tegart, just a boy at the time, remembers his father taking the two erstwhile wild ones, rather than a team of heavy horses, because Rod and Rowdy were typical cayuses — *tough.* The snow was breast deep on the horses and they were pulling a heavy box sleigh. There is a fine photo of them in the museum on this trip for the Richter's.

"Cub" and "Chub," another team of Bob's, were a wedding gift to Bob and Margaret. They were a small, capable team of brothers. Strong and tough, they never gave up on a hard pull, and could get out and trot, a big asset going any distance if not fully loaded. When I first knew them they were in their twentieth year, perhaps older. They lived to over 30 years of age and died within 6 months of one another. They were a big help to Bob in the early years when Bob was trying to make a living with a large family back in the depression years.

There was a Dominion Experimental farm where the current Elkhorn Ranch is located and the families that worked on the farm lived in Windermere. Three families I remember were the Lee's, the Webster's and the Kimm's.

One day while we were caretaking for the Kimpton's I delivered a load of manure to a family by the name of Castle. I had expected to be paid for the load, but instead they gave me a registered Collie puppy. I am sure mother would have preferred cash, but I was happy to have a dog. I named him "Mac." "Mac" got along well with almost anyone, but for some reason he hated Natives. The only reason I could see was that sometimes Natives would go into the barn at the Kimpton's where "Mac" slept. Perhaps some of them teased him.

I enjoyed our time in Windermere, and spent as much time as possible in the saddle. It was while we were living in Windermere that we discovered "Pigeon" had been born at

Little Jimmy's, one of the Kootenay Natives, and once weaned, was turned loose on the range. The government at that time provided the Natives with registered stallions and bulls. "Pigeon's" sire was a thoroughbred. "Pigeon" had the tip of one ear cut off. Little Jimmy used this method, if needed, to mark his stock in the years prior to branding.

One day I was riding north of Windermere, about where the Skookum Inn is now, and I met Little Jimmy riding in the opposite direction. There he sat, an elderly Native with his pigtails, and I knew I was on his horse.

Jimmy pointed at "Pigeon" and said, "Him mine."

I said, "I know, Jimmy, but what do we do about it now?"

Jimmy shrugged and rode on.

Because of the worrying situation in the first years of the Great Depression, I had been allowed to leave school before finishing Grade 8, not knowing or caring then what harm it was doing. However, in 1931 when my father's cousin, May Wreford, was visiting from Devon, England, she was horrified to see me jaunting around with horses and doing field work: hauling manure, bucking stumps, and milking cows. Mother had seen little need in furthering my education and had no intention of paying for any. May insisted on paying for at least one year in Agriculture at UBC. My limited public school prevented me from going further.

While at UBC I boarded with a lady named Mrs. Johnston, close to the campus. I enjoyed my time at the University and my marks were up in the 80's. There were ten of us in the agriculture certificate program at UBC. The only other woman was Margaret Dyson. Social life was pretty much non-existent at UBC and being the depression years, no one had much money to spare for recreation anyway. I don't remember there being many social clubs at the University. I do know that there was a distinct minority of women in other programs as well as in Agriculture.

Margaret's father was the head of Pacific and Yorkshire Insurance. One time he managed to get tickets for the Premier showing of "Gone With the Wind". It was to be quite a gala affair and as a treat he gave the tickets to Margaret for the two of us to go. Needless to say Margaret and I were thrilled at the prospect and got all dressed up and enjoyed the evening out.

Margaret and I were good buddies and I was happy for her when she met up with a young man she had known since childhood, Rolph Forsythe. He had been in Japan for graduate studies on sexing chickens and had only recently returned. When the two were reunited, they fell in love. Because of his time in Japan, Rolph was aware of political rumblings. I think he knew before many of us that war was coming. One time he said to Margaret that he didn't like to see scrap metal heading for Japan because some of it could end up in our boys. Years later when I was working at Woodward's in Vancouver I heard that Rolph had been killed in an attempt to sink the ship Hye Maru on its way to Japan with more scrap metal. I wrote to Margaret to express my condolences. She was touched.

I think I was the only girl competing with the boys at UBC in a ploughing competition with a team. I loved ploughing, especially with horses. Many years later, my husband and I were ploughing the mile long field at Hidden Valley Ranch, Lloyd with an old Cletrac, I with a tractor. Remembering my early days at ploughing with horses, I said to Lloyd, "You know there's one thing I miss at the end of the furrow."

He said, "What's that?"

I replied, "The horses always knew how to go over into the right furrow."

He said, "You wouldn't miss it if you had to rise early to feed and harness them!"

End of discussion!

While I was at UBC acquiring my agricultural diploma, "Pigeon" was loose on Kimpton's 1000-acre pasture at Windermere. When I returned, no one could catch him. It took two Natives a few days to run him down. After that, he was always hard to catch. Finally I used one hobble and two feet of chain on one forefoot, which I changed once a week, to slow him down.

My First Ranch

Nancy and dogs at the B-Arrow Ranch

Shortly after I returned from UBC, Mr. and Mrs. Kimpton returned, and our job as caretakers of the Whitehouse ended. Mother found out from conversations about my riding buddies that Louis Robideaux was looking for a buyer for his ranch, the B→. Louis wanted to return to the States, so Mother bought his 320-acre place on Johnson Road. The ranch came with the assorted machinery needed on a ranch, one cow and a team. We brought along our buggy mare, "Dolly", "Mac" and my saddle horse "Pigeon". Shortly after we moved I bought a bitch to breed with "Mac". She was a lovely Collie that I called "Lassie".

After Mother purchased the B→, she bought a 1933 Chevy from Lloyd Tegart. In those days no one ever locked cars here in the valley. During the summer the four of us drove down to Vancouver. Mother needed a trip to the city, so off we went with me driving. We had a nice trip. One of Joan's fondest memories is of a bear on a leash in Hope. He had a special chair and if you gave the bear a bottle of Coke he would go to the chair and drink the bottle of Coke. Joan loved him.

We went to the show while in Vancouver and left the keys in the car. When we came out the car was gone. The police found the car after it had been driven into a fire hydrant. Our stay in Vancouver was lengthened, as we had to wait for repairs on the car. There was no insurance in those days. It was an expensive lesson for mother to learn.

The B→ was almost completely dependent on horses for transportation. Mother would not drive at night and wanted to play bridge in Athalmer at old Frank Richardson's hall, the first cinema hall in the valley. So I drove our buggy mare along the pipeline, which was up and down over the pipes. The pipeline is now 15th avenue in Invermere. I will never forget my first bridge game. All the Invermere dignitaries were there: Dr. and Mrs. Coy, Frank Stockdale, Mr. and Mrs. B.G. Hamilton, the lady with the only dress shop, and many others. I was quite prepared to sit on the bench along the wall and read my book. The players wouldn't hear of it. I had to play and I hardly knew one card from another. They said, "We will teach you." I drove home that night quite proud of myself for winning the booby prize.

Many horses in the twenties came into the valley from the Prairies, apparently worth more here than there. If these prairie horses ever got loose, we'd know where to look for them, wending their way through the Kootenay Park on their way home. We found that if the mares foaled here they would usually stay happily enough. "Mollie" was a rather ugly, grey, swaybacked, aged mare, born and raised on the prairies. She was brought into the Valley when prairie horses were shipped by the carload and picked up as workhorses by local ranchers.

When "Mollie" came to the U5 Ranch at Edgewater, she was a highly nervous horse, probably ill treated at some time, and she showed an alarming tendency to run away. She did not take kindly to just any driver. I loved her, but my cousin Geoff did not. He was given "Mollie" and her teammate to do a job off the place ("off the place" work brought in much needed cash) and "Mollie" bolted several times with him. I loved her, she trusted me, and over time she worked well for me.

After we left the U5 Ranch in the fall of 1929, I missed her and often wondered how she would fare. When Mother bought the B→, there was a big bay horse that came with the place, much too big and powerful for the work I needed. I remembered old "Mollie". My uncle needed a big horse as a teammate for a black mare for roadwork on the Big Bend, so Uncle and I traded, and I had my beloved "Mollie" back.

"Mollie" was a faithful worker on the B→ Ranch. She surprised and touched me deeply one day. I was hauling firewood in a large hay rack on sleigh runners, coming down the hill toward the house, when a sudden cracking in front of the sleigh alerted me to say "Whoa" before the front gave way, and wood started to pour down onto the team's hindquarters. "Mollie" stood like a rock. I was amazed and still am when I think of it. All she needed was a single whoa from someone she could trust to keep her calm.

I had never forgotten my desire to have a horse like Buster Tegart's. My first "Rainbow's" mother was "Betty", a little chestnut mare I acquired for a bottle of whiskey from Blake Palmer of Wilmer. Horses were hard working creatures in those days and knew the meaning of a rope and halter. If horses had an ill fitting collar sometimes they developed a sweany hole in the shoulder muscle, which was known as a sweanied shoulder. Quite by accident, I discovered a remedy for Betty's sweanied shoulder. Because she was hard to catch, I attached a hobble with a short length of chain to her foreleg, which I changed once a week, just as I had done for Pigeon. In time I saw what the chain had done, the sweanied shoulder muscle had built back up nicely.

In 1934, Bob Tegart and I took "Betty" to Premier Lake Dude Ranch to have her bred to their thoroughbred stallion, "Sun Beau". This mating resulted in my own chestnut "Rainbow".

Farming kept me busy. Between the haying and the irrigation I had to find time for the four milk cows and my horses. We used to make our own butter and cream.

Oswald McGuiness was the water engineer for the Village of Invermere. Paddy Ryan Reservoir was not built at that time and the village got their water off the same creek as the B→. I always suspected that Oswald would watch from the bushes as I turned my irrigation on and then when I left he would come out and turn it off. I had to make many extra trips to turn water back on again.

My life was not all farm work. I took the occasional time off to ride with my friends. Much fun was had at the annual Lake Windermere Fall Fair in the twenties and thirties. It was held where the Athalmer Industrial park is now. I remember one time when Jim Webster, the Swift Meat Company representative stopped in to visit mother and saw a yearling shorthorn heifer that I was fitting out for the fair. He told mother "That is the best fitted animal I have seen for a long time." The livestock competitions included cattle, horses, sheep and pigs. Some came from as far as Nicholson and Parson. There were many stalls set up under cover loaded with vegetables, fruit, baking, preserves, and flowers. Lots of neighbourly rivalry prevailed. It was a major social event as winter travel was often difficult and even summer travel took much longer than it does today. There were some cars, but with the bad roads it was not a fast trip and many people still came with horses. People who travelled any distance came the night before.

I ran "Pigeon" in the Fall Fair races, which he usually won. It was while jumping on him bare back on a side hill at the B→ ranch that my foot slipped on a round pebble that I injured my left knee. No racing at the fair that year, as it came up like a balloon. "Pigeon" figured in another adventure with the cayuses, this time at Island Pond south of Canal Flats where Bob, Buster and Jim Tegart had their eyes on some wild ones, up in the draw east of Island Pond. My cousin Thelma and I went with them. Thelma had come west for an adventure holiday and she got it. This was circa 1934-35, when cayuses were worth more from horse buyers coming into the valley from the prairies.

Bob was usually the only person I trusted to ride "Pigeon". Horses were his living. He worked them hard, but he cared for them well. However, as my cousin Thelma was used to good, well-bred horses in Ontario, she bravely rode "Pigeon." I can't remember what I rode.

We corralled about thirty to forty head. How were we to get them to the Alpine Ranch at Windermere? There were no stock racks for trucks in those days. The men solved the problem by tying two cayuses together about three feet apart.

Thelma must have been shocked at what must have seemed like cruelty to her. Imagine the confusion when the cayuses were turned loose. They were sure they knew where to go. After all, this was their range. It didn't work so well when one horse went on one side of a tree and one on the other. They soon learned. There were five riders to keep them headed north. They were halter broke by the time we headed them into the Alpine Ranch late that afternoon. My share of these wild ones helped me to purchase "Squire Wiggins", an aged thoroughbred stallion standing then, circa 1934, at Lacombe Experimental Station in Alberta.

Around 1934, Mother gave Joan and me $50, a great sum then, to go to the Calgary Stampede. I was determined to bring a pony home for Joan, as I was tired of having to double deck "Pigeon" to take Joan to school when I had farm work to do. I would ride in with her in the morning and she would find her own way home. We had found "Freckles", a Welsh pony cross mare, at a Calgary livery stable. She had an unsightly lump over one eye where she had likely been kicked while younger, but Joan and I didn't care.

We had what I believe to be the first half-ton truck in the Valley. Lloyd Tegart, General Motor's agent in Windermere, had converted an old Star Coupé by taking the rumble seat off and putting a wooden platform on instead. On this, with no sides or rails, we brought "Freckles" home. Mother was certainly astonished. At age 8 Joan soon learned to ride and I was relieved of the duty of taking her to school. "Freckles" took Joan to school, two miles along the old pipeline road.

My mother always seemed to have a male companion when she wanted one. I remember one in particular. Commander Powles was a retired naval man who had a place up on the Radium Hot Springs Hill where he raised foxes. I remember that he had a huge tummy. He used to escort my mother places. One day in the mid thirties, mother asked us girls if we would mind if she remarried. Mary and I were aware who was asking and said that we wouldn't like it. I am not really sure why we were opposed, but Mother didn't marry him. Today I think it would have been better for my mother if she had remarried.

Years of Struggle

My roommate, Francis Jorgenson

We stayed at the B Arrow ranch until mother decided there was more opportunity for Mary in Vancouver and the ranch was sold. Alex Ritchee handled the whole sale. It was not a happy move for me. I had been hoping to breed purebred collies but before I had any pups mothers decision to move meant that I had to give the dogs away. "Lassie" went to Kitty Walker and "Mac" went to Simon Ronacher and his wife who had a ranch on Windermere Loop Road. Years later, when I was back in the valley for a visit after being overseas, I borrowed "Rainbow" from Bob Tegart and rode by the Ronacher Ranch to see how "Mac" was doing.

Parting with my horses was the hardest part of leaving the B→. "Squire Wiggins" went to Bob at the Alpine Ranch 1936 where he sired many really good horses before breaking his leg on the ice and being put down. "Pigeon" went to Hans Jaeggi's housekeeper at the sale. Later I heard that they were unable to catch him and he was sold to a kind Scotsman in Banff who dubbed himself "Minister of Subterranean Passages" — Banff's sewer system. This Scotsman loved "Pigeon" dearly. He said he'd never ridden a horse that could lean into a curve like "Pigeon". "Freckles" went to Hans Jaeggi.

"Rainbow" went to the K2 Ranch with Charlie Webster. He was said to be a very kind man so I thought that "Rainbow" would be safe. Unfortunately, he nearly starved to death during the war until rescued by Bob Tegart. In those days most horses had to fend for themselves in winter. Bob kept "Rainbow" in the barn where he was well fed. "Rainbow's" main job was to take the children to school. One day Bob needed a hard, grain-fed horse for a tough job so he used "Rainbow." The children never used him again. He became Bob's special mount. When I returned for a short visit, I rode him, but had no home for him then.

Alfred, Bob's third oldest child, was small and light and rode "Rainbow" to win many races at the Valley Fall Fair. "Rainbow" died at the Tegart home in Invermere at an advanced age.

I had been raising foals from "Mollie" and had two at the time, one yearling, and one foal at foot. One of the Kootenay Indian Chiefs had a stallion, a grade Percheron, and he wanted "Mollie" to help him raise enough look alike colts to send a carload to the prairies, in order to purchase a pure bred stallion. I let him have "Mollie" on the understanding that when she became past bearing foals, he would put her down. He did not, and I learned after the war that her end was sad. I heard she was broken winded. It still bothers me. I had been in the RCAF while he had her and when discharged, I should have had her put down. I still suffer when I think I could have ended her suffering.

With little education, there were very few job prospects in the hungry 30's. My mother showed no concern for my welfare, and after a frustrating few months, I went to the Okanagan. During a previous trip to the Armstrong Fall Fair, I had met a woman named Dora Blankley who said I could come work with her anytime. I spent a happy year in Armstrong with Dora before returning to Vancouver. I lost touch with my family for a few years at this point.

I worked briefly as a waitress, on Hastings Street near the Vancouver Sun building, before I answered an ad for housework. Out of 50 applicants, I was chosen because of my farm experience. The job was for a Colonel and Mrs. Wright of Wright's Wire Ropes. Their son was off to university for a year and the housekeeping job included the care of his exotic birds. The job paid $30.00 a month, with room and board. I stayed with the Wrights until I was offered $40.00 a month from Mr. and Mrs. Elden Wood.

Mr. Wood was a furniture maker. Mrs. Wood was not well and suffered from anemia, perhaps since the birth of Bobby, their six-month old son. Their son, David, was almost five years old and before long, he followed me around like a puppy dog. David had a bad habit that bothered me. Although he was almost five, he still messed his pants. I asked a friend who was a pediatric nurse what I should do about it. She suggested that the next time it happened I sit him up on a counter so we were eye to eye and very firmly tell him that this was not acceptable. I took her suggestion and the next time David messed his pants I got him up to my level and looking him straight in the eye said, "David, this is not going to happen again." And it didn't.

I stayed with the Woods for one year, working all week with only Wednesday afternoons and Sundays off. I recall Mr. Wood coming home every Friday evening with a corsage and taking Mrs. Wood out to dinner. They were a happy couple. They lived next to the McNut's, Premier Aberhart's married daughter. When I came to leave Mrs. Wood asked me what I had done to David. "He is so good for you and I never heard him cry once." This seemed like a strange comment. When I inquired, it seemed he had cried a lot with his previous caregivers.

I got my next job, with the help of a church minister's wife. She mentioned that there was possibly a position at the Fairbridge Farm School as relief cottage mother for one winter, and was I interested. What a question to ask one of the great unemployed. I knew nothing about the place, but a job was a job. Fairbridge is located in Duncan on Vancouver Island. It was named after Sir Kingsly Fairbridge who was a Rhodes scholar born in South Africa and educated in England. When Kingsly saw the hopeless lives of the slum children in England he gathered private donations to enable him, before WWI, to take a small group of children to Australia where they started what became the first Fairbridge Farm. When WWI came all donations ceased and they were on their own. It was a struggle, but the boys and Kingsly worked hard on the farm they had carved out of the bush. Their effort caught the attention of the public and the Prince of Wales gave his sponsorship.

The Fairbridge Farm on Vancouver Island emerged from this sponsorship. There were two hundred boys and girls aged 7 to 12 when I was there the winter of 1938/39. There were 15 boys or 15 girls in each cottage and one cottage mother. We all ate the noon meal in the large dining hall, but breakfast and supper were the responsibility of each cottage. The children were expected to help out with all the chores.

Some of the children did not know what a bath tub was for when they first arrived. In some flats in the slums of England where there was no running water the bathtubs donated by charities were used as coal bins. One boy in my cottage protested so vigorously that the vice principal, Mr. Bill Garrett, had to physically put him in the water. I think my being a relief cottage mother, meaning I went from cottage to cottage as time off was requested by the full time people, gave a small group of boys the courage to take off overnight for a fishing trip. There was quite a commotion the next day with search parties out everywhere. One year of trying to care for different cottages and never feeling settled with one group of children was enough for me.

When I returned to Vancouver I watched the want ads. One interested me. It was an ad for work at a service station, but it didn't say where, it only listed a box number. I inquired at several stations as to who it might be. One attendant finally said, "Don't say you heard it from me. I think it is Woodward's." I asked Lloyd Tegart for a reference as to my work at his service station in Windermere and I wrote the Woodward's Garage. With my letter of reference I went to the personnel office. The personnel manager was a cold-eyed, uncompromising man. He had no intention of hiring a woman for what he felt was man's work. He wanted to know how I knew it was his garage, but I wouldn't tell. You must remember that this was the mid thirties and any job ad got a mountain of replies. He finally said he would try me out on nightshift maintenance. There were only two women on maintenance, Mrs. Rose, and myself and one of our tasks was to watch every evening as the employees were leaving to check that they were not taking store goods.

I enjoyed working with Mrs. Rose, who cared for the washrooms, and became a dear friend. She told me once that the men's washroom was so dirty that she put a notice up; "We aim to please. You aim too please!"

Another friend I made was a Newfie man who had a crippled leg, He had been at Woodward's for years and helped me to learn how to get through sweeping as I had a whole floor to care for. My Newfie friend showed me how with two 3 foot brooms you did one aisle well every night. You tucked the handles under each arm and wiggled each side in and out to the end where you clapped them both together. At the end of the week the whole floor was clean.

We were doing maintenance the evening of Pearl Harbour, when every light in the city went out. We finished the shift with flashlights. Blackouts were in after that for coastal cities. It was felt that the Japanese knew more about our coast than we did.

I spent the winter of 1941 on maintenance and the next spring I finally got the position in charge of the service station and parking lot. I believe I was the first woman working in public at what was perceived to be a man's job in Vancouver. Finally I got the top work in the Woodward's overhead parking where more care was needed. I was getting $15.00 a week, which at that time was good money - many folks were either making that much a month, or they were unemployed. I believe that clerks who had been with Woodward's for years were only getting $10.00 a week. Writing this now it is hard to believe a dollar then was worth $20.00 now, or more.

While working at Woodward's I lived with a friend, Frances Jorgenson. Frances was working with Dr. Harris, an independent physiotherapist, and he was training her to be a therapist as well. Eventually Francis became a full partner. We both worked long hours and enjoyed our little time off. One of Frances' favourite replies to an inquiry about what to do on a day off was, "Lets have some of Mary's little lamb." Which meant putting on a roast of lamb to have for supper. We enjoyed going down to the beach. We spent many happy hours wandering the shore, looking for shells and driftwood, and watching the birds.

RCAFWD

Royal Canadian Air Force - Women's Division

Nancy at Trafalgar Square

A 3-ton, cab over engine Bedford ration lorry that Nancy drove.

After Pearl harbour it became my ambition to join up. I really wanted to go to England. Although we had moved when I was thirteen, I always had an ache for dear old England. I tried several times to join the RCAFWD. I even wrote to my Uncle Noah in England, who said, "Be patient or come over and join the Land Army." In spring of 1942 I was accepted. I heard months later that Woodward's said they would not accept returned employees after the war, a statement they had to rescind later.

One thing that upset me about the recruiting procedure was the medical. A male doctor gave it, and I was stripped absolutely naked and required to do several exercises. I should have complained about this, but I was so glad to be accepted that I kept quiet. I certainly wouldn't today! At my first medical I was postponed for acceptance because of a bad knee that I had got from an accident in my B→ days. The doctor assumed it would be at least a month before I could pass the entrance medical. With the help of my physiotherapist friends,

I was back in a week and a different doctor could not even tell which knee had been sore. I was accepted. I tell my physiotherapist in Fairmont now that they are not doing what Harris and Jorgensen, registered doctors of physiotherapy, could do in 1940-41. I believe that they knew that the medical profession would limit what they were doing eventually. Some of the top surgeons at the St. Paul's Hospital and the General Hospital used to come to their clinic after 5 PM!

My first stop was Calgary, where I left a trunk of possessions with Mother, Mary, and Joan. We had recently been back in contact with each other. Mary's first job in Calgary had been at a Flower Shop, but now she had a good job with the Federal Government. From Calgary, I went to Toronto and the Havergal College for Girls where training for the Motor Transport Division was held. During my initial interviews where they tested IQ, I was asked to consider remustering as an officer. I was having none of that. I remembered my father being refused officer training because of a varicose vein in World War I and knew I had the start of one myself. Knowing that being an officer would demand hours on my feet, I stuck to my original plan to stay in motor transport.

We were all asked what our desired posting would be and, of course, I said BC. Instead they sent me to Jarvis Bombing and Gunnery Station, Ontario. At the end of the interview at Jarvis with the Women's Division officer, she asked if I had anything to say and I inquired about a chance to be sent overseas, as I really wanted to go. I was told there was very little chance but I insisted that she put my name down. That was in August. In December, working at Jarvis, I was told to get ready to go overseas. Magic words.

In January of 1943, 21 RCAFWD young women from across Canada had been picked to go overseas and I was the only one from Jarvis. Many of the girls, including my transport sergeant, wanted to go overseas as well, and they were all envious. They asked why I got picked; I replied that I had requested it in the initial interview. When I looked right at them and said "Did you ask?" they had to admit they hadn't.

The twenty-one girls picked to go over seas said our farewells back home and then we all met in Halifax. It was one of the coldest winters on record and on the railway trip to the east coast the brakes would seize up a lot. We had to make many stops for "hot boxes" to thaw them. In Halifax there were icicles everywhere, even hanging on the ships.

On the way to England, we young women had a pleasant trip. When we went aboard our ship we realized that it was crammed with Commonwealth Air Trainees, crowded three deep down in the hold in hammocks, on tables and underneath. Unlike the men, we girls had separate cabins, sometimes with only two to a cabin, and we ate in the officers' mess. Knowing the many service men on board were not getting the same quality of food to eat that we were, we started taking fruit to them during the daily deck drills as that was the only time that girls and men met. Many quick friendships were made during drills. The food smuggling soon ended and we were allowed only one each of everything!

We played bridge in the officers' lounge until the passage became too rough and the furniture had to be roped down. Contract bridge was a new experience for me. The ship was alerted by Sunderland aircraft that there was submarine traffic and we had to lie low for two days off the coast of Spain. We landed at Glasgow and travelled by train to London. This was our first experience with total blackouts as we walked through London hand in hand, one behind the other, with the officer leading us with a shaded torch.

We were to be sent to Yorkshire but as Yorkshire was not ready to receive us, we were given two weeks leave with rail passes. I went to Exeter, Devon and stayed with my cousin, May Wreford, who had enabled me to attend UBC for a year. Mae was staying with two friends, because her own house had been bombed. These friends were great travellers and had spent time in Tibet. They had some very interesting souvenirs including a metal jug with a curious spout that went down into the flames and actually kept the fire going when it came to a boil. I enjoyed seeing May and only regret now that I neglected to thank her for assisting me in my year at University. Then it was time to pack my kit bags and go by rail to Yorkshire.

It was cold up there. Our first week did have a few unpleasant incidents, such as "acquiring" irreplaceable ornaments from the Three Greyhounds, a local pub. That was our first experience of CB (confined to barracks) until the culprit owned up.

The air force girls were finally stationed at No. 6 Bomber Group HQ near Knaresbourough, Yorkshire. Our quarters were at Allerton Hall, owned by Lord Mowbrey Sterton. Allerton Hall was a big estate. All the housing was temporary, as it was expected to be used for only about six months. The beautiful carved wood wall was covered with plywood.

It was our first experience of living in Nissen huts. They looked like large oil barrels lying down. We were usually about 16 girls to a hut, with one tiny coal/coke-burning heater. While the officers had coal for their heat, we girls were only given coke. Coke is exceedingly hard to light. Fortunately, every evening at least one girl was detailed to keep the officers' heaters going. In the process, of course, she would bring back some coal for us. Still, coal is also hard to light and we spent hours combing the hedgerows for bits of wood to use for kindling. While at Allerton Hall, King George VI and Queen Elizabeth, with the two princesses, visited and we were presented on parade.

England took some getting used to. There was the weather for one thing. Duty on the runways in the fall in skirts was not exactly pleasant. Battle dress, with trousers, did not come in until later in our time in Britain. What a relief that was. One comic aspect was that our off duty slacks were pale in colour and the English WAAF's thought they were pyjamas. Then there was the driving. I remember my first day in English traffic as if it were yesterday. I was rolling merrily along in open country on a beautiful sunny day, in a three-ton, cab over engine Bedford, with no traffic in sight, when I saw another vehicle on the wrong side of the road. Then I realized, of course, that it was I on the wrong side! I didn't make that mistake again.

There was a minor incident while at Allerton. In my experience as a civilian I had always found it most efficient to take concerns directly to the person in charge. I made the mistake of taking my problem directly to the superior officer rather than go through the ranks of junior officers. This was not acceptable behaviour. As a result I found I was soon posted to Linton-on-Ouse, near York.

Linton was a peacetime flying station that was converted for the RCAF, and had many satellite stations. I soon found that I preferred life in Linton for two major reasons. Partly because I felt my life was more meaningful. Linton was an operational base with Lancaster bombers flying round the clock over Europe. The other nice thing was that as Linton was a permanent station, we had better living quarters, at least compared to a Nissen hut. I was in a small house with two large bedrooms downstairs, one small bedroom upstairs, and a bathroom. Each room had a tiny fireplace that my housemates and I often used to cook our evening meal.

I spent most of my time driving a big 3-ton, cab-over-engine Bedford lorry, making daily ration trips. Shortly after being posted to Linton I arrived one cold morning to find the butcher, an elderly man, trying to get the turkeys cleaned for the Christmas holiday. His hands were blue with cold. This work was no stranger to me, so I pitched in and helped him. From that day the butcher was my friend. Although the country was on strict rations, the butcher would often slip me some eggs or a bit of tenderloin.

My transport sergeant, Frank Martens, was friendly with a hospitable woman in York who always had a houseful of folk, so one more didn't make any difference. I knew her as Mom Laudaman and I would occasionally risk court martial and slip a roast, given me by my friend the butcher, in a haversack to bring to Mom. It was at Mom Laudaman's that I learned the true history of the Yorkshire pudding. Originally it was to save the meat. A serving of pudding the size of a dinner plate was filled with gravy and eaten before the meat was served.

I was thankful for small treats from the butcher because the mess hall was not all that close to our billets. We always had breakfast and lunch at the mess hall and although the food was not great, it was better than most stations because we had Canadian cooks. The British girls were conscripted, we Canadians were volunteers. Approximately

1000 people came to eat each evening at the station mess hall. My roommate and I often used our Billycans to prepare a small meal in our room rather than make the trek to the mess hall. Those were cosy evenings. One evening a girl told a story about her mother's first experience with a water closet. Modern toilets were not common in Britain. She said her mother was distressed because she thought the water was all coming from her. "Every time I pull this chain, water rushes from me." How we all laughed. Another time one of the transport girls got married to the driver of the bomb lorry and when she told us she said, "We're going on passionate leave."

When women left a vehicle, we were instructed to remove the rotor arm to avoid the enemy stealing the vehicle. If anything went wrong, we were to call fitters (mechanics) from the nearest station. We were never allowed to tinker with the engines ourselves. This seemed highly ironic after mechanic training in Toronto!

Mostly I was on the ration lorry, but occasionally I would be detailed to an officer's run. Some days I had to drive a small standard van, which I disliked because the accelerator pedal was so small. Occasionally I had to drive staff cars in London, or in Torquay, Devon. Like all the drivers, I spent much of my on-duty time in the Transport Driver waiting room, waiting for calls to drive anywhere, anytime.

I'd chosen transport to avoid medical problems, but I still had some. Once I went to Equipment for new shoes, but they didn't have my size. So I had to get a smaller size and drove all day to London and back in tight shoes. The result was a bad bunion. I was sent to London for remedial equipment, the most useful of which was an arch support. It was better than any I've had here.

Linton was only a few miles out of York where I found a livery stable. I offered to clean the stables and exercise the horses. The army had commandeered most of the horses, but the owner still had a nice little mare called "Brenda". One day he finally gave me permission to go for a ride along the river. Coming home I spotted a log and thought she could jump it, something I had never done before in an English saddle. Well, "Brenda" dumped me! Fortunately, I was experienced enough not to let go of the reins, which in English riding are joined together, making it difficult to hang on. I made it back to the stables and was happily unsaddling thinking that no one would know, when the owner said, "So she dumped you, eh?" Well of course, the ground is always damp over there. My pants told the story!

I was at Linton-on-Ouse from 1943 to 1945. During D-Day, the Normandy landing, we were all C.B.ed, not knowing what was going on, until our forces had landed successfully. Only the officers were aware of exactly what was going on.

While at Linton-on-Ouse I made friends with a young man named Bill, from Sarnia, Ontario. We used to go in to London on leave to go to the theatre. Bill hoped I would return with him after the war, but our relationship ended while we were still in England. I knew it wasn't meant to be.

A warm friend I made while at Linton was a young woman named Tommy. Her name was Joey Thomson but everyone called her Tommy. Tommy's family, from West Vancouver, had been visiting family in the Shetland Islands when the war started and they couldn't return to Canada. Capt. Thompson was a captain with the B.C. Coast Ship line. While in the Shetlands, Tommy applied as a Canadian to join the RCAF and was posted to Linton.

From Linton Tommy and I were posted to London (Lincoln's Inn Fields, the RCAF Head Quarters) where we were given living out allowances. We were expected to find our own quarters, which we did on Earl's Court Rd. While there, we enjoyed following horse racing via the Daily Express. This started while Tommy and I were on leave in Belfast, the home of the Hospital Irish Sweepstakes. It was pouring with rain as we got off the bus, English and Irish buses had a curved back, where thc conductors could lean over and talk to passengers leaving. We were in uniform, and the conductor leaned over and whispered "Put your money on "Airborne"." Tommy said, "What is he talking about?" I explained that it was a horse running in the Derby that day.

We could have gone back downtown and put our disappearing money on this horse that I had favoured, but we talked ourselves out of it. We went back to listen to the radio at the hotel. "Airborne" won! Wouldn't you know! Anyway, back to London we went and next day to Ascot, clutching the Daily Express, where at the Red Shield Cafe we read the daily Riddle-Me-Ree, a clue to a winner. "Steady Aim" was the clue. Just inside the gate was a racetrack tout who stood on a box offering bets. We said, "What do you offer on "Steady Aim"?" We made a bet and won. We were away now - every day. The fellows, including the sergeant, tried to find how we could pick a winner so often. It was the sergeant picked up the winnings every day. It was all luck. One day we picked a maiden filly, "Heliotrope". When the Sergeant asked whom we picked, Tommy held out her hand like the racetrack touts with a bet. Sgt. told her to go to hell. Of course "Heliotrope" won.

We were in London on V-E Day. It was a beautiful day, and all the office windows were open everywhere and showers of paper were thrown out like confetti. When we were in Edinburgh a short time later, the King and Queen came to a Service Club on Princess Street and we had a nice chat.

After a holiday in Ireland, Tommy and I returned to Torquay. We volunteered to stay on and assist in sending the guys home. We were never told, then or later, of the war grant benefits that would have awaited us if we had gone home at once. If I had known, I would have gone back to school for a veterinary course. I had always wanted to be a veterinary; I already had lots of practical knowledge. I regret this lost opportunity very much.

One opportunity we did not miss out on was seeing a little of Europe before we went home. I particularly liked a trip I made to Paris, France where I had a grand time touring around. Unlike many parts of France that were devastated, Paris was still a lovely tourist destination. I took lots of pictures. I saw the Eiffel Tower of course and Joan of Arcs Statue. Being in Europe really made me appreciate the age and history of my surroundings, but it also made me miss Canada and the open spaces of the Columbia Valley.

Wanderings

Nancy on the Bear's Hump overlooking Waterton.

Tommy and I were discharged August 1946. We both returned to BC, straight to Jericho Beach, where we spent our month of discharge leave with Captain Thomson at Sidney, BC. We later went to Vancouver where we worked in Safeway's fruit and vegetable department. We quickly tired of working at Safeway and having heard that there was money in Angora Rabbits, that is what we decided to do. I had experience in farming, but Tommy had no background in this. Tommy's family were not supportive at first because they did not see farming as appropriate work for their daughter.

Nevertheless, with help from Capt. Thomson and the Veteran's Land Act, we leased 5 acres of land at White Rock. Mrs. Thomson was still in the Shetlands, so Capt. Thomson decided to move in with us. We bought 450 Angora rabbits and settled down to raise them. The rabbits had to be clipped every three months, and this was no problem if you held them upside down by the ears. They didn't move a muscle as we clipped them with hairdressing scissors. We got a young mongrel Collie that we called "Tippy". One time when we were walking on the beach I looked and "Tippy" had gotten a pie somewhere. I called Tommy's attention to it and she said, "Just keep walking. Pretend you didn't see it."

We were just starting to breed rabbits whose fur did not matt (1948) when the Japanese and Italians came back on the world market and the competition made it impossible to operate profitably. We found that we had to sell and we parted. Tommy joined the Red Cross and had a long career as an ambulance driver.

My Victory Bonds, which I had deducted from my meagre pay every month in the air force, gave me the "princely" sum of $500. A lot of money in those days! I invested in a small treed lot on the King George Highway near White Rock. A friend with a bulldozer offered to clear a circular driveway on the lot. This attracted a couple that bought it, at a profit to me! With this, I bought a 5-acre lot near the corner of King George Highway and Johnson Rd., which I still owned in the early sixties. I had an offer on my 5-acre lot, and I sold for less than I should have. I had a dear friend in White Rock that I should have contacted, but being so far from phone and mail I didn't. I can't remember exact amounts now, forty years later, but I know I could sure have done with the extra money!

In the fall of 1950 I returned to the Windermere Valley and stayed with my cousin, Dorothy Brown, in Edgewater. I helped Dorothy with her nine children, and from October to December worked at tying Christmas trees. Fir trees were not cut until after the first frost so the needles wouldn't drop.

Over the past several years I had very little contact with my mother and sisters. Mother would send the odd parcel when I was overseas, and I heard bits and pieces. I learned that in the last year of the war my youngest sister, Joan, had joined the WRENS. My sister Mary was working with the government in the unemployment department and still lived with mother. They were living in Calgary the year I came back to the Windermere Valley.

That Christmas, I was in Calgary at mother's when Lloyd Tegart stopped in to wish my mother a Merry Christmas. I had not seen Lloyd since before the war. I was getting ready to spend the evening with my cousins, Charles and Diana, and

Lloyd offered to take me over. We never made it. It was the beginning of a very awkward romance. Both of us had friends and family in the Valley and we did not want to create problems.

After Christmas, I worked for Brewsters' at the Sunshine Ski Lodge a few miles west of Banff. Back then it was inaccessible except by snowmobile. I took a job as both waitress and housekeeper and since part of the job entailed free skiing, I hoped to learn to ski. Unfortunately, my weak knee kept me from skiing a lot, and one day on the bunny run I injured it again.

There were no condominiums back then, just a little log lodge. I became friends with Thelma, one of my colleagues, who came with me evenings to assist the big Chinese chef with his vegetable prep work. For some reason he had it in for the other girls. Fern Brewster, owner of the lodge, had to sit in the kitchen to prevent him from scaring the other girls with a large kitchen knife.

Some of the guests included an ambassador from Mexico and hockey mogul, Red Burns. We played card games with them nearly every night, especially the newly popular game of Canasta, often until 2:00 AM. During this period at the lodge I remember one young doctor who was still studying. He noticed how much the rest of the fellows were drinking and he calculated that if he saved his money instead of drinking, by the time he finished his training he would have enough to build a house. While I was working for the Brewsters, Lloyd often flew over Sunshine and he always signalled by tipping his wings when he did.

From Sunshine, I moved to Waterton Lakes where I was the assistant housekeeper at the Prince of Wales Hotel. I shared a room with the restaurant hostess at the top of the hotel. From our room we could see down Glacier Lake clear across the Canada / US border. It was a magnificent view. In my free time I went hiking with my co-workers. A favourite hike was just behind the staff quarters. I believe it is called the Bear's Hump. It overlooks the village of Waterton.

Off duty I enjoyed assisting John Russell with his trail rides. John was the brother of Charlie Russell, the famous wildlife writer and mountain guide. John was on contract to the hotel. Good thing the horses were well trained to follow on the trails, as many guests had no knowledge at all of horses. Evenings the jitney dance was popular. Entrance to the dance floor cost each man a dime. Mart Kenny and his Western Gentlemen kept the dancers happy.

Sulphur Mountain was my next stop where I worked with a woman named Donna and her mother. I was horse wrangler cum waitress with the usual added tasks of a small business. We were known as the highest tearoom in the Canadian Rockies. We served coffee, tea and lemon pie. Our regular visitors were the Rocky Mountain Bighorn Sheep. As wrangler, I was in charge of the two horses, a grey faithful mare and a pig headed balky gelding. We had to pack all the food from the hotel at the base of Sulphur Mountain. The water for the tearoom came from a spring half way up the mountain. It is not too hard to imagine the chore that was with one balky horse loaded with water going uphill.

One day we went down to Banff for some grocery shopping and when we returned, we found that a grizzly had broken into the tearoom. The place was well barricaded with wooden shutters and a bar across, but he had broken into the kitchen and licked clean a large can full of sweet chocolate. He had also taken a slab of bacon. When we contacted the warden down in Banff because we wanted a gun, we were told, "You don't need it, that grizzly is travelling." This turned out to be absolutely true, as we never had bear trouble again.

Over the next few years, I worked as a ranch hand in the Columbia valley for a while and spent time at the coast with friends and family. Lloyd came to see me whenever he could. I worked in New Westminster at a veterinary hospital owned by a Mrs. Alson, an English woman who had been a long time rescuer of orphaned or abandoned animals. Mrs. Alson had always had large dogs as personal pets and had been breeding German Shepherds. She was getting on in years and Pete, her husband, felt she should have smaller dogs. Pete was a firefighter, and after a firefighters' convention in Mexico, Pete came home with two Chihuahuas, good ones. Beetle, the little black bitch, would nip my ankle if I tried to stand on *her* chair to clean the window. Beetle produced wee Donna who became not only best in breed, but Champion of the Show at Madison Square Gardens, the largest dog show in America.

If left out in the snow the Chihuahuas would lift their hind legs up in the air and walk on their front legs. It was comical to watch. Donna, who was so small that she could stand on your hand, later became very ill with a virus; she lay absolutely still on a cushion while we hourly fed her beef tea* with an eye dropper. (*Chunks of beef in an earthenware jar, sitting in boiling water produces beef tea). Luckily she recovered.

In 1954, Lloyd recommended me to the Hospital Board in Cranbrook and I spent a year working as a practical nurse. I was accepted as a practical nurse without knowing anything about nursing in a hospital. Joyce Harris became a very special person in my life at that time. Joyce had been nursing there for several years and undertook to show me the ropes. I often worked on the second floor, the maternity ward, which I enjoyed. Holding expectant mothers' hands gave me great pleasure, and I liked working with the babies. I also worked on the paediatrics ward. It was always hard on us to see children so sick. My heart went out to every one of them.

Joyce and I quickly became dear friends and her home became mine too after duty. Joyce's husband had died due to a hunting accident. With five children under 15 years of age, it was a busy home. Joyce was intrigued one day when I suggested Yorkshire pudding as a way to stretch the meat and help fill up her four growing boys, Roy, Terry, Mickie, and John and her daughter Cynthia. I tried rather unsuccessfully to explain how to make it. The oven was not hot enough and the result looked like fish eyes in batter. I tried to comfort Joyce but she said, "Never mind, they don't know how it should look and they are hungry." They ate every morsel.

When a friend, Florence Steele, who lived in Cloverdale, needed some help after surgery, I went down to help. Once Florence's daughter and son-in-law, Terry and Bubs, were coming for lunch. Florence told me to feed them the leftover beef for lunch. I accidentally took the wrong container from the fridge and served them scraps meant for the dogs. I was mortified at the time. Terry's face was a study when, much later, he heard what he had eaten. We had a good laugh. One day, while in Cloverdale, I felt a tremendous pain in my stomach. A short time later Lloyd phoned to say he had been in a bad accident. I feel a bit of background is necessary here.

WWII and its demand for metal had finished Lloyd's General Motors Agency in Windermere, as new vehicles were unobtainable, so he had turned to logging. He made and operated his own portable mill. Lloyd was cutting ties in the valley at his camp on Madias Creek off Kootenay No. 3 Road, north of Fairmont. One Saturday, he was counting ties along the logging road in a van with the windows open, when a 'sweeper', a fallen tree bulldozed on to the side of the road, came in the window and struck him in the chest. Mercifully, the bucket seat fell over backwards. The sweeper jammed the back of the van and stalled the vehicle. Lloyd told me afterward that he thought he could hear a sound like a dying deer, but it was his own breathing. He just wanted to curl up and go to sleep. It was then that he saw a vision of me coming over the hill in clothes he recognized and I said, "Lloyd you can't do that to me."

He managed with one arm to turn the van and go back to where he had seen a man outside his cabin, shaving before going to town. He stopped and just lay on the horn. The only thing he remembers when he arrived at the hospital was Dr. Duthie cutting up his new winter underwear and saying, "You don't move Lloyd." Lloyd replied, "Just roll a log in behind me doctor." His lung was badly damaged. Sometime later when he left the hospital, Dr. Duthie said, "We never expected to see you leave under your own steam." When Lloyd told me this I realized that the day of his accident was the same day as my unexplainable pain in my stomach.

Following this incident, Lloyd was to appear in Nelson for a scaling exam. He flew his own Gypsy Moth to Nelson and passed the exam. He then flew to Vancouver where I met him at the airport. I knew something was wrong. Upon asking he said, "I feel unsteady, when I walk. I am not sure which way I'm going."

I took him directly to Harris & Jorgenson Physiotherapy Clinic at Granville and Georgia. Dr. Harris knew instantly that there was a clot on Lloyd's lung. After several visits spread over two weeks, the clot was dissolved.

We spent a few months wandering through the states. We enjoyed some time with Marjorie and Ray Negly in California. Ray was Lloyd's brother in law. Ray managed the Carborundum Iron Foundry. He made us a wonderful iron pack pan that I still have today. We bought a travel trailer that made traveling home a pleasure. After this trip, Lloyd determined to leave the valley.

I came back to the valley and stayed with Pat and Ned Galbraith while Lloyd made the necessary arrangements for us to leave together. Galbraiths had the campground in Radium that now belongs to Greg Deck. We didn't want anyone knowing I was there, so anytime someone stopped in I would go upstairs out of sight. I suspected that Buster Tegart was on to us as he frequently popped in unannounced. Lloyd finally cut all ties with his home and business and we eloped heading north to the Peace River country.

Lloyd and Nancy on a hunting trip.

Lloyd

We had quite an adventurous trip into country Lloyd had always longed to see. Buster used to tell him about fabulous fishing up north where if you threw a hook from behind a stump and you had a fish

In Edmonton Lloyd bought me the plain $10.00 gold ring, which I still wear. From there we traveled through Whitecourt and on to Valleyview, where I bet with Lloyd on the weight of a pair of Belgian horses. We stopped in Peace River, where Twelve Foot Davis' grave is up on a hill. Legend has it that Twelve Foot Davis made his fortune on twelve feet of gravel. In Manning there was a great Fall Fair. While we were in Grimshaw, Lloyd helped settlers realign the wheels of their vehicles with just a board. How grateful they were.

From the Peace River District we followed the MacKenzie Highway to Hay River, the port for Great Slave Lake. Lloyd nearly went to Hay River in the 40's. During the war, Lloyd had been asked to be steam engineer on the steamer that plied the lake to Yellowknife. Lloyd had always wished he had done it, but at the time had felt than that he couldn't leave his children. There was no road along the lake to Yellowknife, as there is now.

We traveled back to the Alberta Peace River country and decided to go cross-country to the B.C. Peace River country. Roads had been cleared of bush but creeks were not bridged. We "beavered" our way over into country north of Fort St. John by cutting poplars and making our own bridges. Eventually we wound up, via Fort St. John and Dawson Creek, in the town of Prince George where Lloyd obtained a contract clearing railway right-of-way for Pacific Great Eastern Railway, jokingly called Please Go Easy Railway. This was a much-longed-for railway by the early Peace River settlers.

Our first home in Prince George was a trailer north of town, not far from where Lloyd was clearing. Early one morning I felt the trailer shudder. I knew instantly that it had to be a bear pushing the trailer; one shake was enough for me. Lloyd didn't believe me, so I sent him to look. In the kitchen he put his hands on the table and looked out the window and he was looking right into the eyes of a big bear with its paws on the window rocking the trailer. Lloyd grabbed two frying pans, opened the door, and banged the side of the trailer. The bear took off. It was Saturday, my usual shopping day, so I asked Lloyd what we were going to do about the bear. He said to put any food in the middle of the trailer, shut everything up tight, and go to Prince George as planned. "Forget about the bear," was Lloyd's advice. When I returned from shopping, the bear had torn my washing off the line and trampled it. Everything else was just fine.

The strawberries in Prince George were wonderful. They were tiny, but the flavour was out of this world. I made delicious preserves. While we were living in the trailer Lloyd got a bad backache. I asked him to describe it and said that I felt it was his kidneys. I asked him what he was drinking down at the cook shack on the right of way and he said coffee. I knew that it was coffee that had been sitting in a pot all day getting stronger and stronger. I told him he should quit drinking it. He did and his backache went away. The trailer was small and it was so cold that the bedclothes would freeze to the wall. Eventually Lloyd caught the flu and we moved into Prince George to a motel.

After a while we bought a tiny house at 924 Harper Street. This was a happy time for us, even though Lloyd was away so much on the clearing. Lloyd was beginning to feel more positive about life. One time a plumber friend offered to take us to Mexico with him. I don't recall why we decided not to go, but it would have been nice. We wanted to have children, but it appeared that it wasn't meant to be. We even applied to adopt a child but were told our house was too small.

We made trips to Kamloops from time to time and would usually stay with my cousin Diana. We liked to play bridge with Diana and a few of her friends. One trip a bridge partner came by with a white, purebred, Lab puppy and asked if we would like to have her. We called her "Dusty". One trip when "Dusty" was around a year old, we decided to make a stop to see the Adam's River salmon run. We became so engrossed in the salmon that we did not see "Dusty" wander off. When we called her to us, it became obvious instantly that she had been rolling in the rotting salmon. We were travelling with a panel truck. It was a very long trip back to Prince George with a stinky dog.

A small insurance that I had taken out in the 30's, before the war, matured. I was determined it would not just go into the "grocery pot". Lloyd, I knew, would be unhappy if he had to give up flying. He still had his Gypsy Moth that he and his brother-in-law, Jock Palmer, put together in Windermere. In the early thirties Lloyd frequently flew to Calgary on business. The Gypsy was a delicate, fragile plane. All the wood used for the plane had been Sitka spruce. The wings were all wood covered with linen. Originally even the fuselage was wood for this old model. Later a metal fuselage was put together in Lloyd's garage, then assembled by Jock Blakely and his father out on the Windermere airfield, now Jerry Kimpton's hayfield.

I decided to take a flying course that was being offered at the Prince George airport with my insurance money. So, when Lloyd was home on a weekend, I cooked a special dinner and when Lloyd was sitting contentedly smoking his pipe I casually said, "Lloyd, what would you say if I said I would like to learn to fly?"

He was really paying no attention and said, "Okay, I guess."

That was all I needed. Next time he was home I said, "Well I've got two hours in."

He said, "What?"

From then on, he took a keen interest in what I was learning. One evening, after I told him I was doing the circuit before landing and he said, "You are not learning correctly." He insisted on no more money for lessons and he asked who the owner of the training plane was. I said he was in Kelowna. Lloyd phoned and said I would not be continuing lessons. Months later, while Lloyd was searching for a cat in Cranbrook, I finished my flying with Dave Dakin, Treva Burton's brother. I did my solo in the valley from Cranbrook to Spillimacheen and back. My favourite part of flying was the gliding, cutting the engine, for emergency landing after spotting a field.

I completed my training and received my license. We had hoped to have a landing field at the Hidden Valley some day. In the meantime, we felt we could not afford hangar costs for the Gypsy, so Lloyd sold to a young fellow from Pincher Creek, who cracked it up in the Crow's Nest Pass.

Other than a membership with the Prince George Saddle Club, the days in Prince George were sadly to me, empty of horses. I did have friends from the club, Ben Ginter, and his family that kept Arabians and I enjoyed their company. I did have other animals in my life as I acted as a pet sitter on frequent occasions.

Lloyd was often out of town and I needed a diversion other than my business classes and learning in the living room sessions, so I joined the Drama Club. I became friends with Evie Johanson and we were in the chorus for a few productions. Three plays by Gilbert and Sullivan that we were in were The Mikado, The Gondoliers and The Musketeers. Evie later married our friend Per Groland.

Lloyd and I did get active on the political scene. We campaigned strongly and successfully for Gus Henderson who was the Dawson Creek candidate for Diefenbaker's Progressive Conservative Party. Gus had tried several times and had been beaten by only a few votes. He was to be instrumental in getting us established at the Hidden Valley Ranch.

While we were living on Harper Street, Lloyd's wife finally gave him a divorce. Divorces were not easy to get in the

1950's. She kept everything except two pieces of land that she deemed as worthless, the Hidden Valley Ranch and the Old Corby Place.

Lloyd had always loved the Corby Place, because it bordered the ranch where he and his brothers and sisters had been raised. The Corby's raised two sons in the old cabin. Mr. Corby lost his job as teamster, freighting from Golden to Windermere when the CPR Railway came in 1914 and the Corby's left for California in the early 1920's. The Corby place stood empty many years while the Tegart's used the land to water horses and graze cattle. When the government got tired of receiving no taxes on the land, they put it up for tax sale in the early thirties. Lloyd bought it hoping to one day live on it. It lay idle for the better part of forty years. Occasionally squatters settled and every eight or ten years Lloyd's brothers logged parts of it. Overall it was left in terrible shape with the fencing torn down and left scattered around.

During the 50's and early '60's we would come down to the Columbia Valley during break up, the period when the spring thaw makes logging roads unusable in the Prince George area. Down in the Valley all was dry, which made it easy to get into the bush where we did some pruning of our fir Christmas trees. We always camped near the spring, which is up in the northeast corner of the Corby place. One morning from our tent flap we saw two magnificent Bighorn rams standing on the hillside near us.

Lloyd had bought the Hidden Valley Ranch in the fall of 1941. During the war, the bank was going to foreclose on the old Hurst Place, as the Hidden Valley was called in those days. Mervin Hurst had inherited the ranch, but he was serving in the forces at the time. When the bank contacted Mervin to ask if he was interested in trying to keep the ranch, Mervin replied, "No way." Ever since Knudson, a crazy hired hand, had chased him out of the old house with a carving knife and he had been forced to crawl out of a window to escape, Mervin had never wanted to return to the ranch. As Lloyd had expressed some interest in the place, the bank offered it to him. Doctor Coy had advised Lloyd that he really needed to get out of the garage. There was poor ventilation in those days and Lloyd had experienced some chest pain already. He had always wanted to ranch anyway.

Prior to purchasing the ranch, there was one time when Lloyd had gone out to look at the ranch and he found Mr. Knudsen busy digging at the end of the two-story, old log house with a horse and slip pulling the extracted dirt out. Lloyd asked what on earth he was doing and Knudsen put his fingers to his lips and said, "Shh, there is gold down there."

A short time later Mr. Knudsen went to town with two guns on his hips. Bob Pritchard, the provincial police constable, talked Mr. Knudsen into relinquishing his guns and spending the night in the cells. Knudsen had no plans, so Bob convinced him to come with him on the train the next day on a holiday when he left for Kamloops. Apparently when told the train was heading for Vancouver Knudson panicked. The conductor phoned ahead and Knudson was soon wearing a straight jacket. The story goes that Knudsen had deserted ship in Vancouver many years before and traveled inland carrying one oar. He allegedly claimed that he was going to keep traveling until someone asked him what the oar was for. Someone must have asked him in the Valley here, because he stayed at the Old Hurst Place for several years.

We were happy to be able to close the chapter of our life that included no little amount of bitterness, as we were forced to keep our love for each other secret. We made a trip to Kamloops and the home of my cousins Charles and Dianna. We had a quiet church service with Charles and Diana as our witnesses on May 5, 1958. We did not want a splashy wedding. We had pledged our love to each other long before we were finally allowed to make it legal.

We had both missed the Columbia Valley in the years we were away. Lloyd was born and raised there, and I had loved it from the first day we moved there in 1927. We determined to move back to the valley and began the necessary arrangements.

Hidden Valley Ranch

Nancy and "Guard" on the 2010

In 1961 Lloyd was out of work and as there weren't a lot of prospects in Prince George, he left for a few months in the spring. In July I closed up the house and joined him in Calgary for the summer. Lloyd's daughter, Dorothy, was married to Robert Woodall and living in Calgary. Over the next couple of years whenever we were in Calgary we stayed in their old house on the Bow River. They were always most welcoming.

My family was no longer living in Calgary. Mary had been transferred to Winnipeg by the unemployment department in 1953 and Mother had gone with her. Joan had gone to visit friends in Trenton, Ontario and, answering a posting for secretarial work, stayed there. A short time later she met and fell in love with a young man named Bud Jones and on May 2, 1953 they were married. Phone calls and letters were our only contact for a few years. The summer of 1961

Lloyd helped at the Calgary Stampede and worked at Robert Woodall's Cedar Home business. We made frequent trips back to the valley to check on the properties.

In September we spent a month up in Dawson Creek campaigning for Diefenbaker. Upon returning south, we rented a cabin in Windermere and both worked hauling Christmas trees for Hoffert's. We hauled all the trees for Hoffert's that year. "Dusty", our Labrador, would help pull up on the rope, tying down the load. December 8th we headed back into Calgary. That was a very happy winter. We traveled around a bit, but kept Woodall's suite as a home base.

One spring day I said to Lloyd, "I'm going to the races."

"Betting?" he asked.

I said, "I'll place one $2.00 bet. That's it." I had $25.00 that evening.

Summer of 1962 we spent some time at the coast where we both got some physiotherapy. Then July 1st we were back in the Columbia Valley for a wedding and from there began to get Lloyd's ranch ready for us to live there. At that time it was known as the L.T. Ranch because of Lloyd's brand. It is nestled between Steamboat Mountain to the east and the Purcell Range to the west in a natural plain that stretches south from the Francis Creek Drainage. North Hurst Creek flows right through the west side of the ranch. There are numerous fishing lakes within a short distance of the ranch.

Although it was a beautiful location, the ranch needed a tremendous amount of work. Squatter's had left a huge pile of rubbish around the entrance to the old house. We had no money for seed or groceries as we were waiting for our application to Veterans' Affairs for a loan to come through. We had a terrible time getting any Veterans' Land Act money.

Before leaving Prince George in 1961 we had made the long trip from Prince George to Golden on the Big Bend Highway, and then to Cranbrook to apply to the Qualifying Board for money to develop the ranch. We were originally told that we would qualify for funds. Now that we were settled on the ranch, we were told we couldn't qualify for funds to develop the ranch land because "it would fail". The reasons given included the location of the ranch and our age. Lloyd was 60 at the time and I was 46.

In October I wrote to Gus Henderson, the MP from Dawson Creek, telling him the story and he spoke to George Hees, the Minister for Veterans' Affairs. Within two weeks Bill Mackie, the field manager for Veterans' Affairs out of Creston pulled up to the ranch. Bill was a tall man and as he approached the barn where we were gassing up our old Cletrac and a borrowed tractor we had our backs to the gate. We were pleasantly surprised when Bill said "I hear you folks want some money." We were granted $20,000 at 3% interest. That was a lot of money in 1962.

Shortly after that we got a call from Prince George that there was an offer on the house, so off we went. Unfortunately, by the time the insurance and all were paid off there was nothing left for us, but at least we had sold the house. We packed up everything that had been stored there and headed back to the ranch. We had no livestock yet that first winter, so after spending Christmas at the coast we headed back to Woodall's suite in Calgary. April 20th we headed back to the ranch to stay. That first summer mother and Mary came out to the valley. It was good to see them.

August of 1963 Lloyd broke ground for a new house. It was a long drawn out process to build the house as the ranch and livestock always took priority. It was several months with the house being built in stages. We had help off and on from family and friends and a few of the local contractors were hired for jobs like pouring the foundation and building the chimney. You should have seen Lloyd and I when we finally got running water. We were like little kids. The day the tub moved in we both wanted the first bath, after years of washing in a galvanized tub, so we compromised and bathed together.

After the house was built, two men from the Veterans' Land Act in Kelowna came to offer us another loan. They said we had done well, better than most young Vets. Lloyd was so pleased. Unfortunately, we were not making enough to pay insurance premiums. A few years later, when Lloyd died, I had to pay the loan in full.

We acquired a team of skid horses for work on the ranch. “Dollie” was a part Clydesdale mare that I kept with me until I sold the ranch in 1971. Her partner “Chief” was a big 1800 lb Percheron. He seemed to enjoy knocking down the old rail fences. There was a small pasture, near the house that we used for the working horses. It gave Lloyd and I the perfect setup to teach this rascal a lesson. We put an electric wire along the fence, turned it on while eating breakfast, and then watched. “Chief” knew when we were up and around and always came looking for a handout. He took one sniff at the wire and when it shocked him let off a big bang (a fart) and with tail in the air, tore off to the far side, where he stood snorting with flaring nostrils. Needless to say, the fence was not bothered with again.

In the years before we came to live at the ranch the mice, squirrels and chipmunks made hay, literally in any feed or grain at the ranch. Lloyd used to take a sackful of young cats out and just dump them. He could never understand why they didn’t stay. Lloyd didn’t realize that cats, like all animals, needed to be loved. Lloyd’s growing up years had been basically pioneer days. Animals were not pets. They earned their keep and cats were considered expendable. The Statham’s gave us a grey and white tomcat we named “Sam”. When Lloyd would lie out on the couch for an hour after lunch “Sam” would always sleep on Lloyd’s stomach. “Sam” was the only house cat. The barn cats used to come up to the shelf outside the kitchen window for oatmeal porridge and milk

When we had been at the ranch a short time Lloyd asked me if I could train one of the beef cows for milking. He missed what he referred to as ‘real milk’ for his porridge. I was having none of that. Milking a cow ties you to all the cleaning necessary for looking after the milk as well as the regular milking routine. It is cruel to make an animal wait to be milked. I had done my share of milking and cleaning at the U5. One breakfast routine we did start was breakfast in bed. On alternate Sundays we would bring each other breakfast in bed.

Once a week I would usually go into town for mail and groceries. Sometimes Lloyd would come with me. Lloyd commented once that he had always hated mail; it was always bills, bills and more bills. Since we had been together we got interesting and amusing letters along with the inevitable bills. One mail day when I came up behind Lloyd while he was sitting at the table and put my arms around him, Lloyd asked me why we didn't get together sooner. I tried to comfort him saying "Never mind. Our time together has been wonderful and we have done the impossible."

"Dusty" developed cancer in her mammary glands and we had to put her down. My cousin, David Brown from Edgewater, gave us a small Collie pup that I called "Mac" was useless as a cattle dog but he was a good watchdog. He would always let me know when Lloyd was coming home as soon as he crossed the cattle guard a mile away. When Lloyd made trips to Calgary he always came home with a couple of nice beefsteaks. When "Mac" gave the alert I would put on a can of corn and heat up the frying pan and we would have a lovely meal of steak and corn. Once when we went to Cranbrook for a Livestock Conference we left a bachelor friend at the ranch to care for the stock. When we returned he informed me that my frying pans were too clean – the food stuck. I can imagine that bachelors did not wash their frying pans too often.

We worked hard on the ranch and usually only took time off when company stopped in. One time some friends came out to the ranch to visit. Knowing that one of the ladies had always liked Lloyd and made no effort to hide the fact, I said to Lloyd, "Just watch and see, she will get you alone somehow." Sure enough when Lloyd had to go check a pipe out in the field she followed Lloyd and I could see her talking to him. After they left I asked what she had wanted. He said that she had wanted him to meet her in Invermere, alone. Of course he said no. Another time Lloyd told me that if he died I should remarry. I replied "No Lloyd, you have spoiled me for anyone else."

Lloyd and I worked the Hidden Valley Ranch for a few years until a horrible accident in May 1967 claimed Lloyd's life. Lloyd had managed with his General Motors dealing experience to amass a great deal of machinery, a harvester, tractors, and trucks. We kept a large tank of gas to refuel the equipment, but sometimes we filled from the light delivery truck. Early in May Lloyd was out before the sun rose preparing for a trip to Calgary. We had breakfasted early and Lloyd was in the yard siphoning gas from the barrel on the half-ton truck into the three-ton in readiness for a trip to Calgary with two-year old fattened steers. A lot depended on those two steers as cash was limited. Whether Lloyd tried to light his ever-present pipe or if there was a spark, I'll never know. Anyway, gas held down in the early morning coolness exploded, engulfing him in flames. Both trucks were on fire, the ½ ton completely. I started to go to him then went back for a heavy Hudson Bay blanket to put out the flames. I ran outside with the blanket threw it over Lloyd and told him to roll, which he did with his last breath.

When I knew he was gone, I went for help in the three-ton with its back end on fire. A tire blew, and with the speed I was going it put out the fire. I was able to reach my nearest neighbours, Kirsch ranch, with the truck still smouldering. Hubert Kirsch and Bill Pitt helped save the ranch house from the fire.

I stayed on three and a half more years until 1971. After Lloyd died, work on the ranch kept me so busy I didn't have a lot of time to think about myself. There was irrigation to tend, cattle on the range and a house to keep up. I had 150 head of cattle to care for. In 1967 some of them were stolen

Somehow I heard of a group of kids from Radium Hot Springs that wanted to go down to see Queen Elizabeth when she stopped at Fort Steele. The Queen and Prince Phillip were in Canada on a Royal visit and I wanted to see them as well. I had met the Queen while serving in England. I gathered the children and they rode in the back of the truck. On the way home I saw two boys with haversacks walking toward Invermere, so I stopped and asked where they were going. Gene Berglund replied that they were looking for work. I told them to hop in with the kids and I took them home to Hidden Valley and put them to work. Gene, Ken, and Ron came back each summer for 3 years.

When harvesting was done that fall and everything was under cover and the cattle were in off the range, I arranged for a young couple to spend the winter to feed the cows once a day.

I headed to Cranbrook to spend Christmas with Joyce Harris. Joyce was a fellow LPN when I worked at St. Eugene's Hospital in the early '50s. We had remained close friends and she had asked me to come down. A friend of Joyce's sold me a beautiful purebred German Shepard pup. I called him "Guard". He was an exceptionally intelligent dog and was my faithful companion for 10 years.

For nine years in total, I was out at the ranch with no phone, just two trips a week to town for mail and groceries. I often had to rely on my own resources. Once I cut my arm on barbed wire and applied a bread poultice to ward off blood poisoning. The Hansen's were my mainstay for assistance while running the ranch, especially for range meetings. Young Barbara Blakley was also a big help and frequent companion.

Selling the Hidden Valley Ranch was a long-winded business. So many interested, but no money, or they were afraid with it being so isolated. It was far out with the nearest phone in Radium 25 miles away. One Calgary real estate chap came out to look at the ranch and his first question was "Any bear here?" When I said, "Yes" he literally changed colours. I didn't see any more of him!

Don and Carol, real estate agents from Calgary, were frequent visitors. The first times they came I had started taking "Guard" by the collar out onto the balcony. He was very protective of me with strangers. Don said, "I would never question your safety, with that dog."

During these years, I boarded hunters in the fall, and do you think they would listen when I'd say "Don't flush the toilet in the house until I am up and around." The generator being cold was activated by the need for water. I often had to run down to the poor struggling generator to give it more gas!

Two loggers were taking timber off the Hidden Valley, which helped financially. I will never know why Veteran's Affairs did not offer more advice and help when Lloyd died. I could have used a widow's pension. I know that I was criticized for selling cattle that first year when cattle were a good price. The cattle were considered part of the Veteran's collateral. Before Lloyd died we had felt that we could not afford to pay the insurance premium of $300.00 on the V.L.A. insurance, so I owed them all we had borrowed. When I eventually sold, that was deducted before any of it was mine.

After I sold the cows in 1967, I was left with hungry calves. Some of the calves enjoyed the gentleness of a wee roan cow with a huge udder. It was quite something to see her being "attacked" twice a day by at least seven hungry calves. They almost lifted her off the ground as they bunted enthusiastically. This same little cow, when she was calving, if near the house, would look to me for help. It hurt to sell her, but she did go to friends in Wycliffe.

Many were the calving adventures I went through. One black Angus-Shorthorn was so belligerent that I couldn't get near her or her calf. Early spring calving meant calves were often born out in the snow even though I had an open barn for them. One spring this little black cow had her calf near the barn out in the snow. I had to climb up to the loft above the cow-calf scene, throw a rope round the calf's neck, and pull it to safety in the dry shelter. Needless to say, mother was not grateful. She was always a devoted mother to the point of being a nuisance. When she came back from the water hole she wanted back in with her calf. If the gate wasn't open she would go over the fence. I had to watch for the cows returning and rush down to open the gate to the corral. I didn't want to encourage her fence climbing. Her calves always made a top of around 500 lbs. weight in the fall. Fritz Maurer bought her and I often wondered how he coped with her.

Most of the time I was alone on the ranch with little contact with family or friends. Occasional visitors stopped by and at branding time each year Lloyd's brother Jim Tegart and his son Cody Tegart came out to help. I enjoyed having the family out. Lloyd's nephew Happy and his wife Sharon also used to stop out on occasion. In the spring of 1971 I was tired with so much to do and think about and I caught the flu. I went into Invermere and phoned my dear friend Lil, the district nurse, to ask what I should get from the drugstore. She said, "You get over here this instant." She lived in Windermere. I went over and she put me to bed for a week. I could have cried worrying about "Guard", and the cattle at the ranch. Lil arranged for everything. Happy and Sharon were managing the Elkhorn Ranch next door and were commandeered to care for "Guard" and the ranch. What bliss; no cooking, no worries, no cows to feed. I guess I was too sick to worry, but I had faith in Happy and Sharon.

Ranch hands came and went over the years. Some were more memorable than others, just as some were more useful than others. One special hand was a teenage Irishman, John Skrine. John, the son of an Irish lawyer, was here in Canada to satisfy his curiosity about ranching. Remembering my childhood in England and my visions of the Wild West, I truly felt that John and I were kindred spirits. He had the use of my old Volkswagen part flatbed truck in which he ran messages for me to Radium, 25 miles on a winding gravel mountain road. He rode with difficulty due to a disability, but he loved riding the range and helping in the fall round up riding "Kid" my Angle-Arab. Lloyd had always been fond of "Kid"; he said he never knew a horse that would come up to you as a friend.

1971 was the year I sold the Hidden Valley Ranch. How I wish I had sold to an Albertan rancher who wanted it for his grandson. His offer came after I had made a commitment to a group of Americans. I met the Americans on the road as I was hazing some heifers home. Evidently they were looking for the ranch with a wish to buy. I had several offers that year, but the Americans put money down. They eventually bought the place. The Americans, sixty of them that first year, found they couldn't grow a garden due to early frosts and sold the ranch again, eventually going to Dawson Creek. I wish mother could have known about the sale. I know my situation worried her. Unfortunately, she had a fall in May and never left the hospital. She died July 9th. My sister Joan and her family came out to the valley after the funeral. It was nice reminiscing about life in the valley in the 30's.

My first move after selling the ranch was to buy a good GMC truck. With it I could tow my travel trailer and for a few years I lived a gypsy life again.

Olde Corby Place Years

Old Corby cabin pre-restoration.

The cabin, the washhouse, Peter's workshop and the old barn.

Fortunately after selling the Hidden Valley, I had the Old Corby Place. Lloyd had bought the Corby Place at a tax sale in the early thirties after it had lain idle for several years. The Corby's had left for California after Mr. Corby lost his job freighting from Golden to Windermere when the railway came in 1914. In the intervening years Lloyd's brothers logged it several times. And Lloyd and I used it as a Christmas tree farm for a time. It became home base for me during my travels.

In 1973 I, along with my German Shepherd dog, "Guard", spent six months in the United States following the trail of the Tegart family. Lloyd and I had planned to do this together. My trail started with a lawyer-bachelor James Tegart in Phoenix, Arizona. From Phoenix the lawyer took me to his widowed mother, Blanche, in Tucson. I still correspond with Blanche's son Corky and his wife Nila Tegart in Tucson. My trail led from Tucson to Houston, Texas. There was not a rancher among the family. It appears that only the branch that came to British Columbia were ranchers at heart. I made some good friends among the Tegart family in Tucson. From Tucson, the trail led to Texas, where Patricia Tegart McKinley had amassed a great deal of Tegart history, from the Salt Lake City, Utah Mormon microfilms. Patricia insisted that "Guard" come in to the house as well even though the bedroom carpet was white. I used lots of newspaper to try and keep it clean.

Patricia's research revealed that Margaret Fraser, illegitimate daughter of Sir Simon Fraser (last man to be beheaded in the Tower of London) was baptized and registered in the local church. Eventually she eloped with Col. Tagart and a bag of her father's gold to Northern Ireland. His name changed to Tegart, which was the custom if you had a desire to change your name: you changed it when you changed your domicile.

After leaving Houston where Patricia and hubby had made me feel so welcome, I traveled to Louisville, Kentucky in time for the Kentucky Derby. One fond memory I have is climbing a clock tower in the stable yards of the Derby and watching "Secretariat", who became quite famous, win the Derby. I took pictures of the horses being tested for drugs following the race. Unfortunately when I took my pictures in for developing in Toronto the processors lost my film.

En route to Ontario, I arranged a meeting with an old air force friend in New Jersey. Micky had married an American lieutenant during the war and she accompanied me and "Guard" back to Canada. Micky and I went to an air force reunion June 1st to 3rd. We had comfortable rooms, but we didn't see many people we knew from the old days.

We stayed with my sister Joan and her husband Bud in Belleville, Ontario for a day or two, then went to a cabin Micky's family had at Nine Mile Lake in the lake country of northern Ontario and we spent a few days there. "Guard" enjoyed the boat rides. On the first morning after one boat ride "Guard" went missing. I searched for him and found him sitting in the boat patiently waiting for another ride.

After leaving Micky I spent quite a bit of time with Joan, Bud and their daughter Susan. It was wonderful getting to know Joan all over again. Mary was there for a short visit as well. I spent two months wandering around Ontario visiting friends and family. Susan and I made a trip to Ottawa to see the Queen and did a slow sight seeing trip on the way home. Susan is a charming, intelligent girl.

One of my stops was Guelph, Ontario, where my old friend Trevor Jones was living. He had a colourful career that is outlined in his biography "Trevor's Story". I also made a trip out to P.E.I. where Sharon and Happy Tegart were living.

Sharon and Happy were taking care of the largest herd of exotic cattle east of the Rockies. I was able to help with a large cattle sale. It was a very busy day and there was a fabulous banquet style barbeque.

"Guard" and I headed back west in the fall. I still remember the magnificent sheaves of wheat and the huge flocks of geese heading south. It was a slow trip stopping to visit Tegart relations along the way. I spent the winter with relatives in the Abbotsford/Aldergrove region. This was to become the pattern of my life for the next six years. During one of my stays in Aldergrove, I lost "Guard" due to an exploded carcinoma of the spleen after an inoculation for rabies. He died just before a planned trip to Disneyland. I still went, but it was a sad time for me. Several years later, Trevor Jones said that should never have happened, and that the vet should have been reported. I never thought of Trevor at the time.

I spent my summers in my trailer on the Corby Place fencing. What a job that was. The three strands of barbed wire were on the ground, often with young fir trees growing up in them. I had quite a job picking it up, untwisting it, and stapling it to trees as much as possible, though I knew that was not a good idea, as the sap ran out over the staple. In some places recent logging had dragged the wire all over the place. The wire was good quality though and worth the effort of retrieval.

One major hassle in those early years was the building of a road into the place. There had never been a proper road into the place. At the turn of the century the Tegart family and the Corby family were good friends and there was a trail in from the Tegart homestead to the Corby's. It took years of lobbying the government and making a deal with the Natives, whose reserve the Corby Place borders. I even had friends writing the Bennet Government from England and the States enquiring why I was not allowed access to my property. Finally an access road was put in to the edge of the property and I had Hubert Kirsch push a driveway through to my property. I enjoyed my summers working on the Olde Corby Place and my winters working and living with relatives on the coast.

I even took a trip back to England in this time, staying with cousins in Somerset for a wedding, and then with friends in Crediton. The Stevens own my father's old home the farm 'Holwell'. While in England I dropped by to see 'Holwell' and John and Eileen Stevens took me into Crediton, two miles from 'Holwell' where I met John's mother, a wonderful woman named Dot. As I sat across the large kitchen table, that was empty except for a bible in its centre, I met Dot's eyes and knew instantly that I had come to a wonderful Christian home. It has been a great friendship ever since.

In the summer of 1979, while living in my trailer on the Corby Place, my friend Judy came visiting with her beau, Ervin Morneau from Nova Scotia. Ervin was an avid hunter and he asked what the droppings on the Corby Place were. He was thrilled to hear it was elk, as there are no elk in Nova Scotia. After chatting over a cup of coffee, Ervin asked permission to walk the fence. I said, "Sure, let me know if all is well."

When Ervin returned he asked if I was interested in restoring the original old 14' x 16' 1901 cabin. I replied that I was, not realizing that he was in earnest. When he made it clear that he meant it, I stated that it couldn't be at his expense. The cabin was not in great shape. Only half of it had a wood floor, the rest was just dirt and it would need larger windows and a roof. I applied for a grant from the government's Residential Rehabilitation Program that I was accepted for. Over the course of the next year, Ervin restored the cabin on the property to a liveable state for me. He later stated that it would have been easier to build a new one than restore the present one. The four logs on the north side, built up with earth for warmth, were rotten. The other sides were fair; the south side and front had only one rotten log. In the fall of 1980, I moved into my wee cabin and lived there happily sixteen years. Every fall I would go to Calgary for $75.00 worth of coal to see me through the winter.

Peter Tegart is my dearly loved nephew and Buster Tegart's youngest son. I first met Peter at Hidden Valley, when he was nine years old. He was on a visit with his father Buster. Then I did not see him again until we both happened to be at Jim Tegart's ranch in Brisco. By this time Peter was a mining engineer. He was curious to own a horse and I agreed to let him have "Kid" my Anglo-Arab gelding. This led to some happy times with the horses at Boundary Bay where a friend of Peter's had a small farm.

Peter married a lovely woman named Jarmila and I was made welcome at their home over the years while I was "gypsying" around. That always meant so much to me. I was house-sitting for Evie and Per Groland in Golden when Peter's daughter Allie was born. While living at Boundary Bay in the winter I trained "Melody". I would visit Peter and Jarmila as often as possible. Once Peter said, "You know, Auntie Nancy, what you need is a spot of your own, where you can settle for awhile, while you consider your next move." Peter became my partner at the Corby Place.

After we were partners Peter told me that over the years while I was at the Hidden Valley Ranch, he had felt that he would have liked to be partners with me, but felt he didn't have enough finances. How I wish I had had him behind me to advise when I sold the Hidden Valley. I would not have sold the John Deere 2010 with the ranch. What wonderful help it would have been later.

In the days that I was in the cabin water had on occasion been a problem. I was dependent on a well about 30 feet up the hill from the cabin. Sometimes air would get in the pipe and it had to be pumped out, the pump being in the house. Herb Blakley was an ever-present help in these times. Squirrels building nests in the well didn't help either. When I first moved into the place, to stay I often drove up to the creek flowing from its spring to pick up large containers of water. At that time the water was plentiful enough near the road for a bear bath. I never actually saw a bear in it, but the signs were obvious. Peter's partnership provided me with beautiful spring water, piped 8 feet underground all the way from the Northeast end of the 160 acres.

In 1994 I was fortunate to have the property logged by an environmental logger named Don Dehart, the son of Shelagh Dehart, whom I had known at Radium in '28-'29. I knew Shelagh before she married Dino Dehart when she was working at the Blakley's Hotel where I delivered milk and vegetables from the U-5 ranch. When Don came to do the logging I became close to Shelagh and we are still best of friends today. Don did a beautiful job. You would never know the place had been logged. I wish there were more like him. I now had the financial ability to have a lovely, comfortable two-bedroom home. While under construction, Peter called it "Nancy's Palace". To me, it is simply my wonderful home.

There is one tragic note in these otherwise peaceful years. In 1998 I had made an appointment with Garth Brears, an audiologist in Cranbrook, and was going with Carol Clement, who was also a client of Garth's. We didn't check the time to meet at the store in Windermere and they must have left.

I was headed for home, very disappointed and didn't notice the black ice on the hill, south of the junction near Kootenay #3 and the Loop Road. When the van went off the road I was thrown out, as I was not wearing a seatbelt. A truck with workmen that had been following me saw it happen. The van was a total loss. The ambulance came. Apparently I lay in the hospital and they didn't know how I was hurt. Finally I went to Cranbrook where they shipped me by air to Calgary.

I was fortunate to have Dr. Buckley operate on a badly broken pelvis. I came back to Invermere by ambulance in a metal harness unable to move for 3 weeks. Dr. Paul Bach, to whom I shall be forever grateful, saw me through that 3-month stay in the Invermere Hospital. Good physiotherapy would have helped me out a lot sooner. Many people thought I would never leave the hospital, but I did.

Peter has made many improvements to the place. The whole 160 acres is enclosed with smooth wire under tension. He has built a large shed that is a combined tack shop and carpentry shop with a mechanics garage at the north end. This shed has some large windows that have a history of their own, but that's Peter's story to tell. The old barn, built in 1901, was exceptionally well made with dovetailed corners. It was re-roofed and its foundations restored using the existing logs. Peter had a cement floor poured which is a big help in the storage of hay and grain.

Once I moved into my new home Peter and Jarmila fixed up the old cabin for their personal mountain retreat. It was steam washed inside and out, because it was black from the years of burning coal and wood in the old fashioned stove. It is now the tastefully furnished domain of Peter and Jarmila, when they are able to get out for a visit. Between the cabin and the large shed there is now a cute little washhouse complete with shower, washbasin and toilet. What a welcome change from the old biffy behind the cabin.

Nancy and "Dusty"

Winter feeding on the ranch.

My Walk with God

"Guard," my constant companion for 10 years.

Since I was a little girl, growing up in Birmingham, England, I have always believed in God. I was in the Girl Guides when I was eleven years old and once when we had been on a Girl Guide parade our leader took us to a high Anglican service. I found it very different and somewhat disturbing. The priests walking up and down the aisle with incense really bothered me. After coming to Canada my relatives helped us to get the little Anglican Church going in Edgewater. The services were low Anglican. Many were the sleigh rides we had down to the church for a service.

In my years of life at the B→ we would drive the farm wagon into the Anglican Church in Invermere, as our little buggy would not hold mother, Mary, Joan and myself. Wherever we lived, up until I was around nineteen, I attended Anglican services.

Before I joined up with the RCAFWD I was working at Woodward's in Vancouver. There I met a young man who had a great influence in my life. He was the steam engineer for the whole of Woodward's, the garage and the store. So from my position in charge of the parking lot, I saw him quite a lot when he came to check the steam. He told me that he believed that we are Israel. Nationwide, worldwide, we are Israel. He had had a vision while on Vancouver Island. He made the bible live for me. At that point in my life I had turned away from the Anglican Church. It was meaningless to me. His belief in the bible renewed my faith. While in England I searched for a church that understood this message.

I did not find a church that believed in the message at the time and sadly my years in the service were churchless. I spent the next wandering years of my life in search of a church that shared the message that I so strongly felt. While at the Hidden Valley, Lloyd and I tried to obey the word of God and did not work on Sundays. When I lost Lloyd if I had a problem with machinery that I couldn't fix myself I would simply bow my head and call on God. And do you know somebody always came to help me, frequently Cecil Goodwin, or Hubert Kirsch.

While attending service with Barbie, my cousin Dorothy's daughter, in Aldergrove, Barbie said to me "Nancy you are so close to accepting the lord, why don't you raise your hands." I did. I raised my hands and accepted the Lord into my heart. Later in Arizona I met and stayed with some cousins of Lloyd's, Nina and Corky Tegart. They are dear Christians and I spent some happy weeks with them.

During my gypsy years I found a group in Calgary, the British Israel Chapter, where I was able for a time to enjoy wonderful fellowship with fellow believers. Sadly the numbers could not sustain the chapter indefinitely and it eventually closed. I still correspond regularly with a few of the dear friends I made.

Although there are few true Israelite believers in the Columbia Valley, I felt the need for Christian Fellowship strongly, and was lucky for many years to attend a wee church in Canal Flats. Although our numbers were small we had a strong Christian fellowship. The church was closed in 2002 and the congregation has amalgamated with the church in Windermere. The two pastors are Christian brothers and enjoy one another's company.

My pastor from Canal Flats, Bill Doroshuk, quickly became more than a pastor to me. His skills as a handyman were frequently put to use around the ranch. He rarely misses a week when he doesn't call and do any errands I might need. I can't count the number of times I have found his help invaluable. He often finds time for a friendly game of crib and a few moments of silent fellowship.

Sharon Tegart is my dear Christian niece from Irrricana, Alberta. We have so much in common I treasure her friendship very much. We share a birthday, October 28th. Her love of horses may even exceed my own. She also has an entrepreneurial spirit that has led her on many different business ventures. She is a former Stampede Queen and to this day works with the Calgary Stampede office. Although she is a busy lady, she always finds time to call and visits me a few times a year. In one correspondence she told me about a 26-year-old thoroughbred stallion. In her letter she mentioned, "I thought it was only women who had the menopause." She was referring to her husband Happy's acquisition of this toothless stallion, which of course turned out to mean more work for Sharon. Indeed Sharon is never happy without a challenge.

It was very nice that Peter's brother John, a dear Christian from Cranbrook, and Shilo Tegart both came to my ninetieth birthday. Shilo is a flying missionary who currently lives in Riverton, Manitoba. Shilo asked the blessing at my party.

"Sam", Lloyd's cat

"Dusty #1"

Letters from the Ranch
A collection of Christmas letters

Co-author's note

Nancy and I worked together on the first half of this book, rewriting and expanding each time we triggered a new memory. The following letters have been left virtually unchanged. I have added a name or date occasionally to clarify the text for readers who do not know Nancy personally. These letters were sent out to friends and family over the years and although a few have been lost it is a lovely chronicle of Nancy's life from Hidden Valley Ranch days to present.

Sharon Wass

Christmas Greetings 1963

We had hoped to have a picture story of our progress at Hidden Valley Ranch, something we did not achieve, though we have many slides and pictures. Being real honest to goodness ranchers now, we will plan and hope to get our project underway in time for Christmas 1964.

First of all, we are very pleased to report that after a brief period of worry over rain, and hard work with a dandy crew, we were able to harvest a bumper crop of green oats, approx. 330 tons.

Thanks to a Veterans Land Act loan, we now have a nice herd of 107 6-month old beef heifers. Although of mixed breeding, they are a wonderfully uniform lot on the whole, beef to the ground. A few culls will head for market in the spring or early summer, before the bulls go on the range. Eventually, we plan for a good grade and purebred herd on domestic pasture. At the moment, we have ample crown range, but with inevitable losses due to wandering over wide and rough areas, we feel that home pasture is the answer.

After living in a wee 24 foot trailer, we are gradually getting places for a nice home. It will be situated up in the bank above the old homestead, with a lovely view of the mile long field to the south, with a wooded slope to the north behind the house we know it will be warmer than down on the level. Lloyd has been blasting the hillside and digging with an Oliver bucket to make ready for the basement. He has been dumping the fill in a ditch that has to be filled. Through the Veteran's Land Act, I am the contractor, and Lloyd is my subcontractor. Needless to say, we are enjoying the challenge, and learning many new things as we go along. Our planned home will be 26 feet by 36 feet, with two bedrooms, a fireplace, and a wide balcony. All being well we hope, by spring, to be installed in the basement, as the front wall of the basement, facing south, will be framed in with good-sized windows.

Water is a big problem. We have lots of it, but not in the right places! So, for this winter, it is hauling for the house and driving cattle to the water every day. We have big plans in this regard for 1964.

Every improvement, no matter how small, is a great joy, as we love our place and the life we lead. We have put in exactly a year of work here, and are most happy with the results. Folks come from all over the valley to take pictures of our stooked grain, with tickled Lloyd and I to no end.

There will be no returns from the calves until 1965, so logging (with our own timber), and Christmas trees, form our revenue until then.

We have a few future projects in mind. We will put in approximately 6 miles of home fencing and about 4 miles of drift fence on Crown land adjacent to the ranch for our summer range. This is to be done in co-operation with the forestry department who will pay 50% of the expenses. We have a dandy post driver, which helps us a great deal in these jobs as we supply the labour.

As I said earlier, water is an on-going project. We will be filling a badly eroded creek that meanders through the place. The creek will then be put over on the bank that now skirts the ranch, and we can then clear up another 20–30 acres. We now have 85 acres under production, with a possible total of 300 all on the level, ideal for irrigation. One of our big thrills this past summer, was watching our new high-powered sprinkler outfit working. Truly a grand sight in hot dry weather. Mother Nature cane to our aid with lovely rain at the end of June, just in time to enable Lloyd and his two brothers, Bob and Jim, and their men, to put up our south line fence, which effectively sealed out all the range cattle which had been using the place as their pasture during the last ten years. The rain continued on making possible many other small improvements, for which we are grateful, and we never used the sprinkler again. I wasn't sorry, as I was beginning to see those pipes in my dreams.

Our animal friends are increasing. In addition to dear old "Dusty", who will be eight in April, we now have "Lad", a collie whose first birthday was this last October. A small dog (about 30 lbs.), he is a lovely sable and white, and talk about an eager beaver. He would work the cattle all day if he had the chance. Needless to say, he has to be taught a lot that an older dog should be teaching him, so guess who tears across the field to show him with yards of string which we both trip over. Dusty would love to help, but the best she can do is spook everything in the wrong direction.

We had two kittens, Wellington and Napolean, presented to us last spring. Napolean disappeared, whether an owl or coyotes got him we do not know. The mouse problem is no more thank goodness. "Star" a big thoroughbred gelding, on loan from Bob Tegart, is a great joy to me. After a drink of ice-cold water on a cold day, he loves to play. This, if not controlled, could quickly dump one in the snow.

Well, my dears, if you are not completely bored by this time, we will wish you and yours a very happy Christmas. We had hoped to spend Christmas with the Megaw's of Vernon. Unfortunately, the cattle may keep us here. Either way we will have a good rest.

Bless you all.

Nancy and Lloyd

Our bumper oat crop.

Christmas 1964

Since our last Christmas letter, there have been many things happen at Hidden Valley Ranch. As in all endeavours, success mingles with the occasional failure and disappointment. However, at this Joyous Season, we shall just pass on to you our achievements, of which we are very proud. The first is our big ranch sign, which hangs high over the road at our line-fence cattle guard. Mr. Taylor, of Taylor Signs in Calgary, was given a free hand in this project, for which we have received many compliments, so must send him a letter, as I have been meaning to write him all summer! So many acknowledgements are necessary for wonderful services rendered to us this year.

Beginning in the spring, when all life stirs anew, the water runs everywhere and one is ankle-deep in mud, our thoughts go back to the wonderful condition our young heifers were in when turned out this year. They wandered far and all returned safely, for which we are truly thankful. Round-up time this year, with it being a long open fall, could have been a difficult and arduous job, riding in the snow with cold hands and feet. Lloyd was out with a neighbour one day and brought twenty-five head in, but the rest all came in themselves, bless them. Only one, running with a neighbour's wild cow and calf, kept us guessing for a while, but she is now safely home. They are all in wonderful shape, and enjoying alfalfa hay this winter. A few still look for the oat sheaves they were fed last year. Plans in this connection are for self-feeders, which will be filled with ground hay and oat sheaves, making daily feeding a thing of the past. We managed to get one feeder built, but need two more.

Six shiny, black, thickset young fellows were added to the herd this summer with the purchase of six purebred Aberdeen Angus bulls from Vern Downey of Fairmont, B.C. We are really looking forward to our first crop of calves from these bulls, not to mention the revenue! Only hope the price is a little better next year. We feel for the city folk that want a nice steak, but we wonder if, when the price is low to the producer, does the saving go on to the consumer?

The Carlsons of Wilmer, in-between a school contract, managed to sandwich in the completion of the house sufficiently so that it was weatherproof for us to move into, and it really is. The fire will not burn quite often unless we open a window. There are so many things to do yet, but they can wait until spring now. We had a wonderful surprise this summer when the house was framed in. Robert Woodall, Lloyd's son-in-law from Calgary, and a friend arrived, we thought to go fishing. They said they were going to work, and work they did, coming again the following day. In no time, they had the house completely wired. Cecil Gale, our V.L.A. (Veteran's Land Act) construction supervisor, is quite pleased with the house. He calls it "functional", which it is.

We moved in on Sunday, November 1, just about a week before our dear friends, the Lewalls, arrived. Bunnie has been with the survey on the Pine Point Great Slave Lake Railway, and after a two-year stint up north, they are ready for a little easier existence at the coast. How wonderful it was to welcome them to a home where they could turn around without having to go outside! Lloyd and I wonder, really wonder, how we ever stood life in the wee trailer. It is amazing what hope will do for you! One of our big joys in the house is our fireplace. It is going all day and every day. Rubbers, socks, mitts, jackets, etc. dry before it. Stock pails are thawed out beside it. We thoroughly enjoy evenings beside it, reading, sewing, sleeping, and just plain dreaming.

Another accomplishment this year was the successful raising of a pail-fed colt. Not always an easy thing to do. According to general knowledge, it is very difficult to pail raise a colt, yet two separate veterinaries who saw our colt when he was 6 months old could find no fault except that it was noticeable on his knees that he could use more calcium. His name is "Dancer", an honour he no doubt shares with many youngsters this year. I named him "Dancer" after "Northern Dancer" who had just won the Kentucky Derby the day he was born. On a run into town I had taken the time to stop by Allan Tegart's house to catch a bit of the Derby. Allan commented that one of his old man's mares had just dropped a colt that she was not supposed to have and since Bob wanted nothing to do with unregistered horses he was getting rid of it. I jumped at the chance to have a horse and went over to Bob's place right away. It seems that Bob's youngest daughter, Marion, had let an unregistered stallion in with his registered mares the previous fall, which result in an unwanted pregnancy. Bob was furious. Bob had already offered the hours old colt to Wallace Warbrick, but since I arrived on his doorstep first he said "First come, first served", and let me have him. Wallace was very good about it and even helped me load the youngster in my truck. He was a well-bred colt, out of a quarter-horse registered mare that was too young to raise him without stunting herself.

So, "Dancer" came to the ranch in the back of the light delivery, tied down on a bed of straw, before he was eight hours old. The stores were closed and I spent some frantic moments trying to find some baby nipples. I need not have worried; he simply refused to have anything to do with a nipple after the first day! The bucket was good enough for him. Many were the hours of lost sleep while he was small. Feeding times were every two hours for six weeks, but how rewarding he was and is. Full of life, he is never happier than when kicking his heels in the air. He was weaned the end of November and is now on adult horse feed and doing well. He is learning manners already, too, at five months of age. He is halter broken, will get over in his stall, and has been well "sacked out". For the uninitiated among our friends, that is a very necessary and important part of his training, flipping and flapping a sack all over him until he knows it will not hurt him, until he finally pays no attention to it. This pays big dividends in his later training. He not only comes when called, but answers, too.

There are four animal friends in the house. "Lad" and "Dusty", our two dogs, are devoted to one another, but have to be separated for work! "Dusty", a Labrador, packs anything for us with great delight, axes, shovels, pails, etc. are all the same to her. "Lad" is settling down to his work as a cattle-dog very well. He is still over-eager, inclined to be too fast, but when the cows have their calves, they will slow him down a bit! This winter, his big job, and does he ever look forward to it, is watching the big truck while we are loading with feed. He has to keep the cows away from it and he lies at the corner of the barn and waits for the cows to peer around at him. They ignore his warning growl at their peril, as he makes short work of driving them back to what he considers a suitable distance, and then he returns to the barn and lies down again.

One of the projects vitally necessary still is our water situation. We need water at the barns and corrals, not to mention the house! So, if at all possible, this coming spring will see the water coming across the field underground in a plastic pipe. Last winter did see the well cleaned out and recribbed, so that hauling water is a thing of the past, praise be.

Some cross fencing has been done, but very little line fencing, which we need so badly for pasture. Our drift fences on Crown Land have not materialized yet, much to our regret. They are needed in order to turn our cattle out on the only open hills in our area and keep them there until the rest of the range is ready.

We only shipped nine cull heifers this year due to the poor marketing conditions, so shall hope to see better prices in 1965.

We are beginning to feel that Christmas trees are very over-rated, as it takes too much time that should be spent on the ranch.

We have had, as all families do, joys and sorrows this year. Sherry Palmer, a niece of Lloyd's who had just completed her training as an R.N., was married on September 26 to an old schoolmate from High River, Jim Paul. It was a lovely wedding. Her father, though far from well, gave her away from his wheel chair, up in the chancel of the lovely little Anglican Church in High River. It is so rewarding to have these opportunities to get acquainted with the younger members of the family. This happy occasion was quickly followed in November by the passing of her father, Capt. Jock Palmer, a very dearly loved man by all who knew him. First and foremost, he was a flyer. He was a World War I pilot, a bush pilot, and instructor. He and Lloyd, after he taught Lloyd to fly, made a few dollars teaching during the '30's. Jock was Commanding Officer in charge of the flying school at High River during the latter part of the war in '44-'45. He piloted the first airmail plane in

Canada, and was honoured for his exploits two years ago by a Rotary banquet at High River. He founded radio station CJOC in Lethbridge, beginning in his mother's basement, and has made many contributions to the world of radio. He was, right up to his passing, a keen "ham".

At present, it seems we will have to stay here for Christmas, much as we would love to be with the Megaws of Vernon. Reliable folk that are free at Christmas time are hard to find. We cannot close without mentioning the happy times we had this summer when old and new friends and relatives were here. Two boys, Cody and David, helped us with range riding, sprinkling, etc. Cody's little mare, "Mo", was a great favourite.

In wishing you all the best this Christmastide, we will close with those words of inspiration..."A man does what he must, in spite of personal consequences, in spite of obstacles, and dangers, and pressures, and that is the basis of "human morality". — John F. Kennedy, 1963.

Our new sign

Christmas 1965

Here we are again to greet you in 1965 and wish you were here this Christmastide to visit with us and look out at our long field, as it stretches a mile from one end to the other. From our windows, we look down about three-quarters of it. How we do enjoy our home, even though it is far from finished. The fireplace looms large in our enjoyment, though Lloyd does "blow up" sometimes if it smokes, which it does occasionally. We seem to have a downdraft problem, which often occurs when a house is on a hill, so we have been told. Eventually I learned how to place wood so there was no smoke. A large piece of thin wood placed in the front with the fire lit behind it seemed to draw the smoke. Kurt Carlson, who built the house, is hoping to be able to come and work on the finishing in the New Year, which will be eagerly anticipated.

This year has seen a start made on our long-awaited water system and we hope by the time you receive this that our cesspool and water in the tap will be a reality at last. Personally, I can't wait until that first lovely drop of water comes out of the tap, and I know Lloyd will feel the benefit of no more pails to pack. "Dusty", our nine-year old Labrador, will be puzzled no doubt. She often took pails down to Lloyd at the well if they had been forgotten. The yard looks, at time of writing, as though a cyclone had struck it, what with huge mounds of earth and trenches all over the place. We are hoping that the well will be sufficient for the house and barns and have pipe running both east and west to barns and a short line north to the house. Now water will be available to the bulls and calves from the one tank, half on each side of a fence. The bulls and calves will be sharing opposite ends of a barn, one of the nice warm log buildings that are still in excellent condition, after forty years. The horse barn and main corrals will also have water. What a difference this will make to the care and condition of the stock. Anyone who has chopped water holes, and watched stock straining to reach down, afraid of falling in, will appreciate fully what this means to them and us. In order to get the water pipes laid, we had a back-hoe here, working every weekend for a month, and our little John Deere did a dandy job of pushing the earth that Tom Marr and son, Andy, so laboriously shoveled out, back in again, on top of a generous bed of sawdust, both above and below the pipe. While all this was going on, the only way to get across the yard was to leap. The horses just snorted and stayed put, though it did not take them long to pick their way along a narrow strip to the barn where there just might be a handful of oats.

This year saw our first calf crop, something we have been eagerly awaiting. The heifers will not be three years old until next spring and for that reason, they were bred to calve late this year, so, of course, the calves are mostly small. However, in spite of this, we were pleased with the price received. Next year, all being well, we should have some nice early calves. We are culling strictly again this fall on the basis of calf performance and general ability to do well. Shipping days at Hidden Valley Ranch are quite hectic, starting as they do long before daylight. We arise early enough to have breakfast and be ready to start handling the animals, feeding, etc. before the brand inspector arrives. Then there is the loading, always a nerve-wracking job for Lloyd and I, as we pride ourselves on having our stock trusting and quiet, so that the necessary chivying to drive them up the chute and into the truck upsets us as much as it does them. A few of our beasties still get south and when they are picked up by neighboring ranchers in the fall, the men know ours instantly because they are so gentle and unafraid. They know our trucks and come looking for a handout, even in the middle of the summer, when we are checking them on the range. When the truck is finally pronounced secure and ready for the road, we both feel as though we have done a day's work and yet, for us both, it is only at the best, half done. Lloyd has a long, slow trip to Calgary and I have the herd to feed and water. During earlier shipments, when the cattle are grazing on the field, I go with Lloyd.

Winter has come early this year. We are feeding two weeks ahead of last fall, though up until the end of November anyway, they still go out rustling every day, after feeding. The light snowfall so far has enabled us to feed all over the field, so that we can get certain spots well fertilized.

A big whitetail, five-point buck has successfully eluded would-be hunters this season and is now safe for another year. He crossed our field regularly, over the fence, across the road and up the hill, narrowly missing hunters several times. Lloyd also had his eye on him for our larder, and the day the big fellow presented an easy shot, Lloyd missed him. Poor Lloyd, he just could not believe it, a standing shot. On examining his rifle, which he had taken with him on horseback the day before, he found that half the rear sight was gone, which, while it helped his hunter's pride, did not fill his craving for venison for breakfast. Elk crossed the field often at the lower end, too, until their lord and master was taken. They were not seen again. Hunters are a big worry to us every year and when this young bull elk was taken, we caught the hunter in the middle of the field our cattle were grazing in. We took the elk and turned it over to the game warden whose hands were tied because we had not erected "No Shooting" signs. So, the case came under simple trespass, the fine at the moment is a maximum of five dollars. No wonder the stockmen and the Farmer's Institutes are continually pressing for stiffer penalties.

We have added twelve more acres of new land to the production of crops, and managed this year to save a bumper crop of oats grown on this land. Last year, it was impossible to save the oats. It just poured and poured and we were forced to cut the bands and let the animals in. What a wonderful month they had and it certainly gave them a boost for the winter. This year, we had this new land fenced, which made a dandy fall pasture for the bulls. Last year, they had to run with the herd far later than they should have done, so each year sees more goals reached and passed.

Our stock-rack was another goal. We had needed it for so long and now that we have it, we cannot imagine how we ever got along without it. I never realized how many bolts were needed for a stock-rack until I helped Lloyd with ours.

"Dancer", our palomino pest as Lloyd calls him, has grown so well this past year that few, including a veterinarian, will believe he is not yet two years old. We have been so busy that I have not had time to give him any training, other than to make sure every so often that he does not forget what a halter is for. I have seen so many otherwise well-broken horses pull back and break their ropes that I am sparing no effort to make sure he has a healthy respect for a rope. There is a borrowed surcingle in our bedroom closet; that means a new experience for him one of these days. A bridle and some bitting hours are in store for him shortly. He still comes when called and wants to kiss me whenever I approach him. This consists of rubbing my face and nose with his upper lip and then putting his nose up high in the air with the most ecstatic expression one could possibly imagine. I often wonder how long it will last!

"Lad", our two-year old collie, is settling down to business now and is more content to walk when driving. He does not approve of being asked to help when the cows have calves, for which I do not blame him. Nevertheless, it is a big help just to have him with you. They know it means business when he is there, even if he is at heel.

We had a surprise early in October when a Frenchman that we knew up at Chetwynd dropped in on his return from a trip home to France and stayed to cut Christmas trees for us. A little unexpected revenue is always welcome. In the spring, with the help of a brother of Lloyd's, fifteen hundred ties and six truckloads of lumber were manufactured and hauled to the railroad and town. This timber removal makes the clearing of more land possible.

A huge D7 cat has been added to the machinery, which we hope will help us to clear land and do some logging. Lloyd, the "dickerer" that he is, got it for a song, really; otherwise, the place could not afford it. In fact, our good friends of the V.L.A. would be quite dubious about it were it not for the fact that we are quite isolated and have a tremendous potential in land development here. A new square hay-baler and side-delivery rake were added to the harvesting equipment, which was a great improvement over last year when Lloyd was away a month during haying on an exchange deal. A similar situation had to be avoided this year.

The year 1965 had its joys and sorrows, as it does with us all. Donna Tegart, a young niece of Lloyd's, was married in a lovely ceremony in the little Anglican Church in Invermere. It was at this time that we met Sharon Patterson, a former Calgary Stampede queen, engaged to "Happy" Tegart, a well-known bronc rider, and nephew of Lloyd's. She is a lovely girl, a horse-lover, and trainer of barrel-racing horses, so they should have a great deal in common. Their marriage was in Calgary on September 18. The passing of a dear friend, Bob Mcgaw's father, saddened November for us. He was out hunting, which he loved so much, on the hills near the ranch. Would we could all pass on as quickly and peacefully as he did.

In spite of all we have managed to do, there is still a tremendous amount of work necessary before the place is doing anywhere near what it is capable of. Many people are interested in it, especially Americans, and as Lloyd and I would like to have a little comfort and leisure before we depart this mortal coil, it is quite likely we will sell, provided it is worth our while.

No record of our doings at Hidden Valley in 1965 would be complete without mention of the assistance rendered by two young men. Cody Tegart, a nephew of Lloyd's, who with his good little mare, "Mo", was responsible for bringing in some of our cows and calves in October and November. Michael David Brown, a young cousin of mine, worked well and mightily with us all summer and takes a real load off Lloyd, especially when water is needed at the house. They get along fine, both being mechanically minded.

It is time to close this, I am afraid, rather lengthy epistle and wish you all the best this Christmas time. I have a wee thought that a very dear friend sent to me years ago, which I pass on to you with love from us both:

"I suppose the important thing is not what we get, but what we do with it, or how we do without it."

E.H. Young

Christmas 1966

How time flies, the more so it seems as we get older, and here it is, time to greet dear friends and family again.

This has been an exceptionally busy year at the ranch. In fact, as we develop, we find more and more needs doing, instead of less, as we had so fondly hoped! For instance, the drift fence, from the end of our Southeast line fence east to the Steamboat Mountain rock bluffs, a project that we need desperately to accomplish for the saving of feed and our hay land in the spring, just seems impossible to do. Our forestry friends could well take us for a pair of prevaricators on this score. Several times we have planned to get at it, but sometimes this place reminds us of a very busy beehive. One would think being over twenty miles from the nearest store and telephone, that life might easily get dull and that we would long for town and company. Not a bit of it! We don't get the chance, as there is always something or somebody turning up in connection with ranch business. Our friends know that if they arrive during working hours, it's a quick cup o' tea and on with the job. Then supper and a good round of bridge, especially in the long, dark winter evenings, with a good fire blazing in the hearth. We can honestly say that since we came back to the ranch, we have been so content with our lot and our way of life, that it is an effort quite often to go into town for mail and a few necessities every ten days or so. When the time comes to leave here, we shall miss it terribly, we know.

The timid, graceful deer trust us enough to raise their fawns where we can watch them play in the long summer evenings. Our family of huge, black, glossy ravens, who resented us so bitterly with continuous raucous cawing when we first came back that Lloyd threatened several times to shoot them, are a definite part of the ranch today. We would miss the soft swoosh, swoosh of their wings as they make their daily inspections, looking for mice, etc. If anything is wrong with an animal, they notice it at once, and so we learn to live with nature and appreciate its creatures. To get back to the drift fence for a moment, we still hope, to at least get a start on the bridge over Frances Creek, which runs through the easterly part of the ranch. This is a prerequisite to any work between the ranch and Steamboat Mountain, and precious time was spent just in the selection of a suitable place for a crossing.

Our young cows, now in their third year, have given us a nice bunch of husky crossbred calves, mostly black whitefaces, which we plan to feed through the winter. Last year, we put a small bunch through on good alfalfa hay and a small oat ration, as they were late calves. They did so well this spring when marketed that we are taking a calculated risk on all of them this year. Where or how we will meet our numerous bills this winter will be another question. We hope to get some tie milling done and logs for nephew Allan to haul to town. Our friends, the Annis' of Suffolk sheep fame, gave us all a boost last Farmers' Institute meeting by having some dried beet pulp lined up near McLeod, so shall be watching the calves progress with extra interest this winter.

Milk Weed or Timber Vetch, for which science has no remedy up-to-date, has been troubling us. A few cows every year seem to fall for it, some in fact appear to be addicted to it. These animals, unless caught soon enough and put on a complete change of food, go down hill in flesh rapidly and lose their milk. All this adds up to orphan calves. Some of the older ones manage to suck other cows when their calves are feeding. We imagine this is where persistence pays off, as the unwilling foster mother finally gives up trying to bunt the little intruder away. The odd one or two that we feed in the yard during the summer become real pets and are quite an asset when weaning time comes. Their quiet "what on earth's the matter with you?" attitude as they eat and contentedly chew the cud, seems to have a calming effect and gets the unhappy babies onto their new feed much faster, we feel.

Any time that we can spare from the livestock and farming work is put in on logging in order to get more land cleared for hay and pasture. We were quite proud this spring to see Allan Tegart, hauling our 43' spruce logs with his huge Hay's diesel. The loads averaged 8,000' and kept young Henry Veenstra busy crawling all over the end of the logs, putting our timber mark on in red chalk. Colleen, Allan's daughter who was out helping me bake cookies (which I loathe doing), would watch from our kitchen windows, high up on the hill, and when we heard the big diesel roar up the coulee, we'd hurry to get Allan's meal ready and Colleen would try to persuade her dad to let her spend the night here instead of going back to help mother in town! These spruce logs were the product of last winter's work, and their falling, bucking and skidding has opened up new land between two fields. The cows ate the spruce needles all winter and bedded down on the limbs. Any one who has ever known the sheer delight of a bough bed on a camping trip can understand how much our cows appreciated their beds last winter. Every day after feeding and watering, they would wend their way up to the logging. Sometimes they would be in the way, but it was over-looked due to their obvious enjoyment. We plan to do the same thing this winter if all goes well, as this land above the buildings, up the draw toward the mountains, is truly wonderful land, rich loam with not a rock on it. When cleared, these fifteen acres or so will join in one long field (about two miles) the two homesteads that comprise Hidden Valley Ranch. Since returning, we were fortunate to obtain another 160 acres through the old Land Settlement Board. The original Hurst homestead, where the buildings are, was 320 acres and the Snook place, further up the draw, 200 acres. The old wagon road up to the Snook place went through the Hurst yard almost. Actually, it was up on the bank outside the yard fence and went along the bank on the same track that we are now using to the basement of our new home on the hill. Our plans envisage two roads, or two levels for access to the house. The upper one, nearly completed, will run along the back of the house and give access to the two side balconies, one to the back door and the other to the wood box for the fireplace. This is an innovation we are both looking forward to seeing in use. The wood will be piled on the balcony and be handy for keeping the wood box filled. Needless to say, this will have to be very carefully done and in the summertime. As yet, we are not too sure how to proceed and are wondering how many of our friends would have any suggestions.

Our water supply here is excellent, but depends to a great extent on the work we are able to put into it. Hurst Creek, which runs through both properties, is our irrigation water and has always been ample for our needs. With new land being prepared, we have to make sure that we have sufficient water, especially in the fall when snow-fed creeks tend to dry up. This year, we managed to do something we have wanted to do ever since coming back, and it turned out to be both rewarding and exciting. One beautiful fall morning, early in October, we loaded the John Deere crawler tractor, which is equipped with a bulldozer blade, onto the big truck and hauled it about three miles up a forestry access road which skirts the ranch and into the bush a mile to Hurst Creek. There, we proceeded to bulldoze windfalls out of the creek bed. It was tough going, many of the logs proving too much for the crawler, necessitating some chainsaw work. Things progressed fairly well the first day until nearly quitting time, when the left track came off the John Deere, half in and half out of the water, and the chainsaw decided to bind in a wet log! About this time, home was beginning to look pretty good! We would have liked to have had the big old D7 on the job from the start, but it was too far to walk it and our truck is not equal to the job of hauling it. Next day, we took off with two dogs, "Lad", our collie, and a boarder, "Rinty", an Alsatian belonging to friends from Invermere, and proceeded to get the track back where it belonged, which was done in short order. Soon we were down far enough so that Lloyd decided to work the big cat up along the creek, and when she turned, ready to put her huge twelve foot blade down in the creek, that was a pretty thrilling moment for us both. I climbed in with Lloyd, and away we went, pushing a small tidal wave ahead of us. Huge trees left by a logging outfit while we were in Prince George lay across the creek, but with so much power, they just groaned and gave way. Triumphantly, huge piles of debris, bush, and smashed logs were deposited high up on the bank and we almost sailed down the creek. Lloyd said it reminded him of the riverboat days when they used to put scows in front of the sternwheelers on the Columbia River.

This year, 1966, saw so many additions to the ranch that it is hard to say which brought the most pleasure. Amongst our animal friends, we sustained the sad loss of "Dusty", our white Labrador, following an operation, which proved our worst fears, cancer. Her place in our lives is still empty. "Sam", a gray tomcat, full of character, at home as much in the rocking chair as he is anywhere on the ranch, has helped to fill "Dusty's" place in the house. At the moment, there is a battle of wills going on. He is determined to sally downstairs to the unfinished gravel floor in the basement. I am equally determined that the back door in the kitchen is the only one he can use! A sweet-tempered thoroughbred mare, "Trouble", and her half-Arab colt, which we have just registered, were an added enjoyment to me this summer. The young fellow is now partially weaned and already walks into his quarters at night, eagerly looking for his handful of oats and minerals. We were very fortunate to get this lovely mare literally for a song, as the owners wanted a good home for her. "Dancer", our palomino stallion, received some much-needed discipline when "Trouble" and her baby arrived on the scene. He has had some training this year and is quick to learn, but pressure of more vital work has prevented any steady riding, which he must have this coming spring and summer if he is to do his share. He is as well grown and developed as most three-year olds now, and yet will not be three until next May 16th, the day "Northern Dancer" won the Kentucky Derby, which was how we came to have him, hence the name. Before we leave the horses, I must mention that Lloyd has asked for the colt to be called "Kid", so in the registration, we hope they will give us the first choice, "Ibn Annfar's Kid", "Ibn Annfar" being his sire. "Ibn", we discovered, means "son of" in Arabic.

Machinery, that vital part of today's farming, was increased by the addition of one of the new Hesston swathers, which really cushioned the haying strain for us this year. It does a marvelous job of cutting, crimping, and fluffing up the cut material so that it cures evenly and leaves it in a swath so that picking up by the baler is accomplished easily. No need for raking any more, except in the event of rain. One has quite a position sitting up there above the crop, almost like a cab-over engine deal, with levers similar to a cat for guiding it. Lloyd is using, with great satisfaction at the moment, a new John Deere 2010, four cylinders, which presents a decided improvement in power and ability to do the job. With our heavy snowfall, a good three and a half feet packed, we could not exist out here without it. Needless to say, the logging and clearing will, we hope, justify the expense.

Our narrative tends to grow longer each year it seems, and yet we cannot close this without noting briefly a few measurements of progress: our own generator for power, lights, and water. Robert Woodall and a friend took time off on a fishing trip to finish the putting in of the lights. What a wonderful day and night that was, lights on Hidden Valley Ranch. Per and Evie Groland, from Golden, arrived one Friday evening in October and spent all day Saturday helping us put the tile down. How wonderful the living room and kitchen look now. A vacuum has been added, a gift and a great joy. No more tea leaves needed now to keep the dust down. The woodpile is moving further away from the house. The first winter we were in the house, the yard wasn't fenced and the cows slept on the sawdust and chips, etc. beside the basement! The big D7 has been traded in on the new John Deere, but is still here and so Lloyd was able to do most of the work on the road at the back of the house before the snow fell, and also, he put in a dandy new road, straight and wide, from the gate. Now we can look from the kitchen window, past the gate, and right out to the flat, where the cattle come in the summertime, so that we know they are there and can go down and check them.

At last, after three days and nights of the most awful cries of grief, our newly weaned calves are quiet and peace has descended on the ranch once more. Occasionally, one who has worn her voice into a piteous wail decides to try again, but even the cows are quiet now, so all is well.

In closing, our real wish is that we could see you all at Christmas time, but as that is out of the question, we will be thinking of you and wish you all the best for Christmas 1966 and a Very Peaceful and Prosperous New Year,

From the folks at Hidden Valley Ranch

Christmas 1967

It is with a very heavy heart that I greet you this Christmas tide. My darling husband passed to his reward in May, during a terrible accident here on the ranch. The main thought that kept me going afterwards was Lloyd's love and dreams for the ranch. I couldn't let him down, and the pressure of crops and animals, their care, and the need to supervise the young fellows that I had with me for help, kept me going as I am sure nothing else would have done.

Lloyd's numerous nephews and nieces, who have always given us their love and help, rallied around and have been such a very real source of comfort to me.

We endeavoured this year to pasture the cows and calves on the field, but the alfalfa was too much for them and we had to eventually put them on the range for a very short while. The upper field, the old Snook homestead, which was still in clover and timothy, held them for a few weeks and was a big help.

Haying was excellent this year. We had as dry a summer as I remember back in the 30s. Inexperienced young men handling the irrigation pipes did not help matters, but our hay was in beautiful green bales. The forty head of calves that I have been feeding this fall, due to go to market the end of November, really look forward to their nightly feed of good green alfalfa and come up from grazing in the big field on the dot of 5:00 p.m.

"Dancer", our three-year old palomino stallion, is broken now and at the moment, awaiting plans for his future. He needs something to do, something to put his teeth into! What it will be, I do not know at the moment. In other words, he is still "a problem child", albeit a loving and beautiful one! "Kid", the young Anglo-Arab stallion, is a horse of another colour! Gentle and grave, but a livewire on occasion. I have been riding him already and he was only a yearling on June 10th of this year, but is well grown for his age. He took the bit as though born to it. His mother, "Trouble", has had a marvelous summer running with a thoroughbred stallion and his harem up in the hills at The Royal Antler Ranch. "Lad", our collie, and "Sam", the cat that Lloyd loved so much, are welcome companions, especially "Sam". Anywhere is okay with him. "Lad" has forbidden areas, such as corrals, etc. unless called for special occasions, such as getting difficult cattle into corrals. Even though he is getting older, he still would like to hustle the cows faster than I allow!

This fall has seen a veritable hive of activity around the ranch. Lloyd and I had strung 1,000 feet of two-inch plastic pipe across the field to the corral last spring in order to get water to the stock from the springs, but it had to be put underground. So, Robert Kimm, of Kimm Construction in Invermere, came and dug the ditch with his backhoe and now we have running water all the time in the corrals. He also took the high bank away from the bathroom window and made a start on the road past the house on the upper level. Per and Evie Groland, old Prince George friends now in Golden, came out weekends to help put the balcony/carport up. Great excitement in the middle of November when the eight-inch posts from the bush were raised to support the balcony. Friends dropped by to say hi, but we put them to work before gong in for coffee! All the posts went up in jig time. Leroy got the chainsaw going, too, which was most important at the time.

At this moment, we are busy getting wood in for the winter and fixing the big stock tank with an overflow pipe, and general winterizing. It is a very real pleasure to have this precious liquid flowing through the corrals instead of going over and chopping ice for the animals at the creek. It represents a very real improvement for the ranch.

Jim Welfare, a young man of 18 from Vanderhoof, arrived only a few days after the accident and was a real tower of strength all summer under very difficult circumstances, not knowing ranching, local conditions, or people. He is now taking a welding apprenticeship with Andy Cochran of Colchester Supplies, Grandforks, who sent him to me in the first place. Seems fitting somehow. "Liza", one of our Shorthorn cows, who gives a nice drop of milk, was named by Jim and raised four calves all summer. What the future holds for our beloved ranch is difficult to tell at this point. Two men are interested in it, with a view to raising horses, which would please me if either goes through.

What a wonderful, long fall we are having, the first since we came back here. It is such help before the winter. Lloyd said it was like this in '41 when he bought the place.

We had a lovely surprise one evening when two very dear friends from Prince George days (now in Victoria), Kay and Bill Tidy drove up to the house. Bill is a wonderful photographer and took pictures of "Kid" and the place. Robert and Pat Megaw, from Vernon, also took some grand pictures of the place in May. These pictures are now in Milwaukee with a prospective buyer.

Every year, we have to pay tribute to the kind assistance of friends and/or family. This fall, Henry Newcomen, a nephew of Lloyd's by marriage, came late one afternoon and hooked up our generator, which now lives in the small log lean-to on the old log house. This was such a great relief and help. Then later, during the hunting season, Bob Megaw and Gil Suter were here and worked wonders, joining old electric wire together, putting up poles, and we had lights in the barn and haymow. Its value was not fully realized at first, but when I wanted to work on two calves one night, what a blessing it was to have lights and be able to do it after dark.

In closing, I ask God to bless you all, and give one and all a very Merry Christmas and a Happy New Year.

Queen Elizabeth at Fort Steele

Christmas 1968

I find it very difficult, especially at this time of year, to enthuse over happenings, events, and accomplishments on the ranch that has meant so much to us both for the past ten years, and to Lloyd, for many, many years, in fact long before he bought it in November 1941. I know though, in my heart that he would wish me to carry on as before. He did so enjoy the yearly resume of our achievements, and the interest that all our friends showed in it pleased him so much.

Looking back to a year ago, the thought that seems uppermost in my mind is the wonderful co-operation the ranch has received from so many people in all walks of life. How I could have continued, alone, so far from everyone, without this grand help, I do not know. God bless them one and all, and may their shadows never grow less.

I do realize now that the place is too much for me and I have put it up for sale. The ranch has come close several times to changing hands this year. In any event, I hope and pray that only those who will appreciate its beauty and possibilities will purchase it finally.

Livestock, always to me the real core of ranch life, has seen an increase from last year when I felt that, due to all the extra time that had to be spent in settling the estate, I simply could not do justice to both crops and cattle, and so my small herd, badly depleted by this time due to circumstances beyond my control, went to market and I was left with three small, late fall calves (one black crossbred Shorthorn heifer and two steers) and "Liza", the wee Shorthorn cow that friends had for the winter for her milk. Needless to say, she is not wee any more. In her year away from home, she has grown into a huge, blocky cow. Tug Hansen and his wife and small daughter arrived today, November 25th, with "Liza", and she was turned loose in home pastures once more, with her daughter and nearly thirty head of young stuff I picked up at the Cranbrook sales this fall. The weather has been, and still is, wonderful, with just sufficient snow to prevent frost damage, so that the steers and heifers are having a long grazing period, which is a very real blessing.

I enjoyed my first experience in purchasing cattle very much, and for several reasons. All the sales staff were very kind and so many of the local people, many of them retired, who had been buyers, were buying for neighbours, were most helpful. From the first Cranbrook sale early in September until the end of October, I only missed one sale and during that time, brought many small, undernourished calves home, which, after a few weeks of grain and intensive care, have really flourished on our good fall pasture. Several, you would hardly recognize. The last four, about three-week old Hereford steers, soon caught on to the daily routine of out to pasture all day and into grain, plenty of good alfalfa hay and a warm, sheltered spot to sleep. One has a wee bell, and its evening tinkle is the sign that they are nearing home and if they dawdle too long, "Guard", my constant companion, tells me it's time to go and get them in. Though only just over a year old, he shows signs of being very intelligent with stock, which pleases me very much. He is a purebred German Shepherd, a strikingly marked, large and handsome dog. He was three months old when he came to me on January 1st of this year, and he has accompanied me in my winter travels, which helped me so much I am sure to recover sufficiently from the loss of Lloyd to carry on here at the ranch. Before leaving the cattle, I must mention the few head of really nice Shorthorn and Hereford heifer calves I bought in Cranbrook. They are so far ahead of what can be grown up in this area that I feel they were a good investment. Now, before they enter the winter, they are as large as grain-fed yearlings were last spring.

We had one of the best crops in the valley this summer and thanks to a hardworking nephew of Lloyd's and his wife, Charlie and Jean Kohorst, their son and numerous young helpers from the Edgewater area, the hay was put up in jig time. Sales to pay for the work were hauled from the field to Golden and Lake Louise. A huge stack soon reared its head above the stack-yard fence, and although it was all sold in short order for a very good price, it was a satisfying sight, after all the worry and hard work of the summer.

Our young red chestnut Arabian, who was gelded this summer, is a real joy. I have ridden him several times and though he is so gentle at all times, he has all you need under the saddle, too. He is a beautiful sight to see when he feels the cool evening breeze and wants to warm up a bit. With his tail, a red plume over his back, he floats with a long, graceful stride from one end of the field the other. When I leave the ranch, he leaves with me. Lloyd loved him more than any horse he had known; therefore, he is special. His mother, the brood mare, "Trouble", is here and I hope to get her in foal again in the spring for a prospective buyer.

"Dancer's" fate still awaits him and at the moment, we wonder whether it will be here on the ranch or in the Okanogan Valley. A friend of many years ago turned up in my life again this year. Kay Milligan, as she was then, was at UBC when I was there in the 30s. We were both in agriculture and she came and assisted me on the B-Arrow Ranch out of Invermere one summer. From there, I thought she had gone to Montreal and we lost track of one another until this summer when going through the valley with her husband. She enjoyed a ride in Golden and asked Billy Foyston who was in charge of the horses, and who used to ride with us around Invermere, if he knew where I was. He told her that I was at the Hidden Valley Ranch. What a grand reunion that would have been, as we had been so close to one another in '32. She was in the Airforce, too, and at Jarvis, only a few weeks before I arrived there. However, she was destined to stay in Canada, while I went overseas.

This year, a good friend and neighbour, John Lynde of Dunbar Lake, a few miles north of us, assisted me to insulate and install the large stock tank that Lloyd and I bought in Calgary. Now water flows continually, with the overflow being piped into the lower corral where water is often needed in the summertime for various reasons. So many hours of hard work every winter are eliminated now, we hope. There is no future in cold water for your stock, young or old.

Just a few days ago, our friends and perennial hunters, Bob Megaw and Gil Suter, left with their bag of whitetail bucks. It is so wonderful to see them every fall and the ranch is always a more comfortable place for them being here. This year, the automatic choke on the light plant was not functioning properly, so the banker and the fabric man did what otherwise good mechanics could not seem to figure out. Now she is running merrily again, much to my joy and comfort.

Two hunters from Vancouver Island, who were hunting from the ranch as paying guests, had me tearing over to the plant in the dark, right out of bed one morning, because they had used the bathroom and not followed wilderness rules regarding the water. The poor plant was struggling to pick up, without choke on a cold, cold morning.

I hope to be able to go to the Megaws for Christmas, all being well, but actually until the place definitely changes hands, I do not feel easy in my mind about leaving, especially in the winter.

So to all of you, wherever you are, A Very Happy and Peaceful Christmas is Hidden Valley's wish for you.
With love to all and may God bless.

Nancy and "Dancer"

Christmas 1969

This yearly Christmas message from the ranch, which is an effort to do so long before the joyous event, is nevertheless something I always look forward to with keen delight. On reflection, I know the real reason is because Lloyd always enjoyed it so much and was its most enthusiastic supporter. It is the memory of this that makes the writing of this journal of Hidden Valley Ranch activities a continued joy.

This past year has been an exciting and eventful one. To all of you who are wondering whether I am still here, the answer is "yes", though events in July and August seemed destined to terminate my life at the ranch. However, it seems that I am meant to stay and care for our beloved home for this winter anyway. When it seemed that I would be signing all Lloyd and I had worked so hard for away in a few days, I felt quite drained. After the initial disappointment had worn off, I discovered that I was relieved and happy to stay.

Looking back to early spring and summer when the labour of getting water on the hayfields is foremost in one's mind, I fully realize how blessed we were this year. There was so much rain that it is the first time since we started here in 1962 that we have not had to put the irrigation pipes on the field. Conditions were getting very hot and dry shortly before cutting started, but it was too late then, and the only thing left to do was hope that we could get the water on right after the hay was off. Ranchers in the main Columbia Valley, but a few miles away, had most of their crop cut and partially baled (we are a week to ten days later, due to altitude), when the rain started, and did it ever rain! For three weeks, it literally poured, causing dreadful losses in spoiled hay. Many ranches were forced to haul the heated and rotten hay to coulees and draws in order to get it off the fields so that the second crop would thrive, which it did, watered as it was from the heavens.

With the assistance of a young man from Calgary and two younger from Kimberley, all my crop was safely gathered in. These young men, toward the end when there would be days they were idle, would take the tent and spend a few days at Radium, enjoying the pool and the delights of feminine company. It was a wonderful arrangement and if I do have to continue through another season, I am hoping we can do it again.

Negotiations on the sale of the ranch have taken a different direction from last year. Its value for recreation is being promoted, with several parties being interested, and the difference in price is a great inducement to carry on and should enable a very good return on our investment. Although fully realizing the potential value of the place for recreational purposes, I certainly did not ever think that we would be able to benefit from it at the present time. Needless to say, the Easter holiday spent by our Prime Minister Trudeau, and the honeymoon of Nancy Green Raine at the famed Bugaboo Spires, only eight helicopter miles from the ranch, must have given this whole area a great deal of publicity, and certainly quickened interest in the ranch.

In the animal world (my great joy), there have been many changes, some with a touch of sadness. "Dancer", my problem child, returned from the Cranbrook area where he had undergone training to be under the saddle and work. Once back to his familiar haunts where he knew how to open every door and gate, he spent a carefree two months becoming friends with "Kid", the chestnut Arab three-year old. His trainer in Cranbrook expressed disappointment that he would take no interest in his work. Seeing the change in him since his return home, I feel sure that he was simply homesick. In May, he went to work leading trail rides at Radium, which he seemed to enjoy as long as he was working, but standing with nothing to do was not his "cup of tea", so when business slackened off, he came home. It was obvious to me that he had to be kept busy, which I was unable to do because of the workload on the ranch. Through a friend in Calgary, "Dancer" is now in the possession of a young man of sixteen who goes on long trail rides and has the time and the love that this five-year old palomino quarter horse needs.

"Kid", the gentle Arab, who asks nothing more than a scratch on the chin whenever I am near the fence and comes on the gallop with his tail, a plume, held high, will likely be starting a new career shortly. I shall miss him sorely, but it will only be a temporary separation. Sharon Tegart, a niece, who is a horse trainer, has a young English girl that she has been coaching who recently fell in love with "Kid". So Sharon plans to train both in the arts of the show ring. As a matter of fact, we are hoping that "Kid" will restore Wendy's belief in the equine species, which has been badly shaken by her first acquaintance with a horse that had to be corralled before it can be caught!

If the Arab, with its centuries of living in its master's tent, doesn't do the trick, I'll be very surprised. "Kid's" mother, the thoroughbred mare, "Trouble", is, we believe, safely in foal again to an Arab. She appears to approve of the Arab, as last year's attempts to unite her with a thoroughbred stallion and the previous year with "Dancer", proved unsuccessful. She is now with Fred and Lorraine Miles at Marysville, near Kimberley, on a "share the foals" basis. This gives me happiness and peace of mind, as she is in good hands and still gives me an interest in horses, whether I am at the ranch or not.

"Kid" gave me a wild ride a few weeks ago when, after fixing fences all morning, we were coming home up the big field near the road. He was pulling at the bit, wanting to run, and as we were loaded down with a Swede saw, hammer, axe, extra wire, and a bag full of assorted items, such as staples in a tin, pliers, etc., guaranteed to make plenty of sudden noise when exposed to the vibrations of hard gallop, I was in no mood to indulge him. Then I heard the sounds of a vehicle approaching from behind and above us where the road is ten or twelve feet above the field. Instead of turning the young fellow around so that he could see what was coming, the next thing I knew, he had taken a giant leap forward and was on his way! It was a moment or two before he responded to the pressure of the bit and he was brought back perforce, to have a good long look at "that horror". It was one of these nice new jeep vehicles, closed in and so comfortable to travel in, owned by Mr. and Mrs. Baum (he is an American writer), who purchased a home near Radium last year. They were on their way out to the lakes to do some fishing and promised to stop in for a chat and a cup of tea on their way home. All this, of course, after they had recovered from the shock of seeing what they at first thought was a runaway. Needless to say, so did I.

Cattle have really been coming and going this year at the ranch. A nice bunch of mixed heifers and yearlings went on the range and did very well. Most of them are in, thanks to the efforts of Sharon Tegart, a niece, and Fritz Maurer, a neighbour from Windermere. Snow has held off so far, which is needed to track the last ones out. By the middle of November many of the animals had been marketed, but I still am going down to the sales at Cranbrook, taking yearlings and bringing small calves back. The last trip was an especially enjoyable one, as owing to the kind effort of Walter McKersie from The Thunder Hill Ranch at Canal Flats, I am the proud owner of a 1969 GMC light delivery truck. Oh, how wonderful it is to have some power again, not to mention the joy of back-up lights and heat! I have not parted with the little old faithful Volkswagen. I would have had to almost give it away, but now it will help to preserve the new GMC by doing all the rough work around the ranch for quite some time. I also have a sneaking hunch that I may still be very glad of the wee "wagon" again this winter. They are simply wonderful in the snow.

The field above the buildings that I call "the spring field" (as the small creek fed by the springs flows along its southern boundary) has been added this year. Lloyd and I were working on this every moment we could spare, as it was Lloyd's dream to have the two meadows, the old Snook homestead, which comprises the upper north-west portion of the ranch, and the spring field, made into one meadow. His dream has become mine and working the John Deere tractor-crawler piling brush and pushing out stumps on this truly beautiful land has been a real joy. There was not one rock and the depth of the soil was fantastic. I am still burning the twentieth day of November and if the snow and cold weather holds off, I shall try and finish the ploughing, which is about three-quarters done. At the moment, this ploughed area is the daytime haunt of the smaller calves, who, led by the perennial "Betsy" (I always seem to come home with at least one calf that has been someone's pet) with a small bell, wend their way with "Guard's" help, up to pasture in the morning and back to their feed and barn for the night. They enjoy digging around in the soft soil, especially where there are some black stumps. Their white faces are a picture at times when they look at you so solemnly.

Logging, commenced by A & B Logging last fall, has opened upper slopes for pasture, and the alluvial flat for further hay fields. At the time of writing, the sturdy little John Deere is busy making skid roads (carefully chosen so as to not harm the natural beauty of the creek area) to enable bringing logs across the Frances Creek to their new mill set on the hidden east side of the hog's back, which runs along the center of this lovely parcel of land. Many men have seen this as a delightful spot for summer homes, especially for ardent fishermen. It doesn't take many minutes to catch a nice mess of trout in those big, deep pools under the logjams. The line that Bunnie Lewall, a surveyor friend from our Prince George days, ran for us last year between Lots 7907 and 9444 was a real blessing when Bill Perron and I were down by the Frances Creek looking the situation over before they move down in the New Year to start logging there. Now is a good time to get roads in, before we have too much snow. The next problem will be keeping snowmobile riders from trespassing once an area is opened up. I hear that the local snowmobile club is busy making roads for winter fun further north, of which I sincerely hope they make good use! I have given some thought to catering to snowmobiling parties here at the ranch, as we have such a wonderful depth of snow all winter, never less than 3' packed. With the lovely, long hayfield, almost a mile long, it should be a snowmobiler's dream, especially for anyone with children. The worst that could happen to them on a fast run would be a dunking in the snow. I am glad they did not take me up on this as any action on the fields, even over the snow, can burn the grass.

The hunting season this year brought many joys in the form of new friendships through old ones. When Bob Megaw arrived one Sunday evening, he really had a surprise package with him. His mother-in-law from White Rock, whom I first met and enjoyed so much when Tommy and I were in the Angora rabbit business at White Rock in 1947, was sitting there in the car. That was, to me, a wonderful week, though what her impression of a supposedly quiet and restful spot was, I am sure I shall never know! There was not one day, I don't think, when we really had time to talk. People were coming and gong all the time. It seems to be "either a feast or a famine". Since they left a week ago, except for the loggers, I have had the place to myself and I am sure that if it was not so, I would not be getting this letter away in time to my friend, Eve Bergman, in Calgary, who always faithfully gets it done for me, even if I am late getting it in.

I cannot close this message without some mention of the animals about the house. The two dogs, "Lad", the seven-year old collie, and "Guard", the big German Shepherd, who is just past two years old, complement one another perfectly in my needs for their services. "Lad", who could never be trained to stay with us unless we were constantly on the move, stays at the house, warns me if there is someone coming, and keeps the bear away from the house. In this connection, people seem to be surprised that having bear so close does not seem to bother me. Lloyd would never harm them as long as they did not bother us, and with a dog, you have no problems. One evening last summer, the two dogs were growling on the back porch and looking along the bank toward the barn. It was just getting dusk and I saw what I thought was a black stump, but it moved. It was a black bear quietly feeding. They know how far the dogs will allow them to come and I enjoy seeing them around. "Guard" has always, from the start, been my constant companion. It is a rare occasion when he does not accompany me; so rare, that when he is left behind he is usually tied to his kennel for fear he will try and follow me. He is a great help with the cattle. His only fault is youthful enthusiasm! He had one licking when he drove cows into the fence and now he never needs anything but my voice. The small calves know when they see him coming that it means business and head for home in a hurry!

The two cats, four-year old "Sam" and year old "Pepsi", do an exceptionally good job of keeping the rodent problem under control. They are so much more pleasure for me and they are happier themselves since I had the cat shelf installed at the big kitchen window where they eat and sleep if they wish. Though "Sam", at any rate, usually prefers to sleep in the hay. I can't help feeling that the next occupant of the kitchen will be more likely to use it for a flower box. Needless to say, the cats and "Guard" enjoy the fireplace with me in the evenings. "Lad", an outdoor dog, would not thank you for such luxuries, and in any case, it is good to know that his sharp ears are on duty at all times. He has very definite ideas on what is all right after dark, he lets me know at once if a vehicle is approaching, nearly a mile away. His bark warns me before the lights can be seen, as a rule.

This has been a wonderful year for the people and events that have occurred at the ranch. It is impossible to mention them all here, but their visits are all recorded in my daily diary. One party stands out particularly just now in my mind, as I have recently received in the mail a book I have always wanted to read, Eric Collier's "Three Against the Wilderness". I was just finishing up some tail-end baling one afternoon in late August when I saw a car draw up on the road to the ranch and who should step into the field and start taking pictures but Roy Ferguson of Calgary. His kindly, welcoming smile must have warmed the hearts of many in the Adams Wood and Wieler auctioneer's office at the stockyards in Calgary. He and his wife and two friends from New Hazelton, in northern B.C., spent a most enjoyable afternoon with us and took Ken, one of the boys from Kimberley, to join his pals at Radium. It was Margaret and Jack Strathern who so kindly sent me the book that I am looking forward to enjoying by the fire.

I must close now, hoping I haven't wearied you, with the most sincere wishes for A Very Happy Christmas and the very best of health and contentment for 1970.

Special to the Tegart clan wherever they may be. It is, and always has been, wonderful knowing you all. So full of personality as you all are, but as George Ross of Ghost River Ranch, Cardston, Alberta, says in his column in The Free Press – Oh boy!!

May God bless all of you.

Christmas 1970

I am writing this year's letter after two bitterly cold days, watching the snow falling gently and the cattle rustling contentedly in the big field. I am anxious about the few head still out in "the boondocks" somewhere. Hunters come in and will, perhaps say casually, "Saw nothing but a few head of cattle today", completely ignorant of the fact that domestic animals, with the exception of horses, are not supposed to be out on the range this time of year! To me, on thinking it over and discussing it with friends, it is simply that we are becoming fast, an urban-minded nation. Before the war most people understood and appreciated rural folk's problems, but not today. I am planning a bit of a campaign through the press and hunting clubs to acquaint hunters with this very real need for their co-operation. They should inform the local ranchers when they see cattle at large in the fall. I think they might find that it could be a two-way street. Ranchers would welcome them and perhaps make hunting privileges more available. My friend, Bob Megaw, on his usual hunting safari, got his whitetail buck while assisting me looking for cattle. It was quite a thrill to be with Bob and able to assist him. It was dark before we had the trophy buck cleaned and into his dandy Volkswagen bus. The extra weight was a blessing, as the snow was deep enough to be a problem.

Life on the ranch this year has been a continuation of the past three years, with my concentration being on making as good a sale as possible. Lloyd, understandably, wished it to remain as a ranch, and so it may stay, as there are parties who want it for that and are willing to pay the higher recreational price. The daily work on the place is carrying on and I am endeavoring to do what I know Lloyd wanted done. The upper half of the place is now under fence, making grazing available under controlled conditions, which is a great asset. While fencing this northwest portion of the ranch, I discovered a beautiful spring, which would have really thrilled Lloyd had he known. Water has always been a problem, particularly after the Hurst Creek dried up in late August, but this spring opens a new dimension for grazing in the fall and spring. An application, granted by the Water Resources at Victoria, on Frances Creek above the place would, when developed, give necessary water in dry years for development anywhere on the place.

Our Highways Department bridge crew is the doubtful recipient of black thoughts this fall. When any work whatsoever is done on or near the bridges, homecoming cattle will not go over them. Four years ago, Lloyd and I, with the help of Bob Megaw and Gil Suter, two hunter friends, tried everything possible to coax cattle over a bridge that had been re-decked a few weeks previously. Finally, we had to go back to the ranch, six miles, and get hay for bait. Even then, it was touch and go. Later in November this year, bringing a small herd home, a bridge, in the process of being widened within four miles of the ranch, was a barrier they would not cross. Fortunately, Joe Kirsch from the Kirsch ranch, our only neighbours, brought his old dairy cow down with an armful of hay, and while she fed contentedly on the bridge, we pushed ours on and over. What a relief!

My wonderful GMC half-ton truck has done a lot of work this fall, hauling cattle home. It means many trips, but it is so comfortable and reliable. It is a real boost to my morale after two years with the little old Volkswagen. The snowmobile is coming into play on the cattle finding in the fall. Alfred Tegart, a nephew of Lloyd's, covered the Height O' Land area on Sundays late in November looking for strays. In this connection, I'm seriously thinking of getting a snowmobile myself. One or two lost animals would just about pay for one. One of my heifers, a two-year old, stayed out all winter and had a calf, her first, this spring. A bought heifer, she is inclined to be wild and so I'm wondering whether we will get her in this fall or not. I may have to ask someone to shoot the calf for winter meat. It would not survive, and sucking all winter, would pull the heifer down in flesh. I often wonder how many people sitting down to a nice juicy steak give a thought to the tired, wet, frustrated ranchers who made their meal possible.

This year was the first year my chestnut Arab, "Kid", has done any serious work. We drove the cattle for two days in

June, pushing them north from the Height O' Land to the drift fence at Elliot's Flat, also known as the Nine Mile. Then late in August, I received word that my shorthorn bull had damaged himself. So "Kid" and I got him in and I hauled him to a neighbour's for examination and to be close to the vet, who comes up from Creston once a month. "Kid" handled himself very well and loads and unloads out of the truck like an old-timer. He will be joined this winter by a half sister, out of his mother, the old thoroughbred mare, "Trouble". Her name is a misnomer, as she is the most gentle of mares! Jim White, an old-timer of the Fort Steele district, had her as a pet. She would come in and eat tidbits off his table, and he used to say, "You're nothing but a trouble!" "Melody", as the young filly is named, is also sired by an Arab, so it will be interesting to see how she develops, and I will have a nice mare to breed someday. "Kid's" plans for this year were solved, as Wendy decided that she wanted to own her own Arab.

Of great interest to all valley folk, especially the Tegart clan, was the filming of the Walt Disney film "Ole Hacksaw", produced and directed by Larry Lansburgh, on location at Lake Enid, just west of Wilmer. It is the story of a thoroughbred stallion that serves on a chuck wagon team, driven by Tommy Dorchester, one of the greats of chuck wagon racing. Sharon and Happy Tegart were doubles for the stars, Sue Bracken and Tab Hunter. They did all the potentially dangerous acting.

The hay crop was reduced this year due to two things: my lack of foresight in not ensuring that the mill set used by the two men logging here was put across the creek, rather than between the creek and the field, and the unusually dry year. The combination cut our crop almost in half. However, with a huge stack of 1969 hay still in good condition, it matters little, really. The dry year makes prospective sale of this hay look bright.

My cattle population is governed mainly by the necessity to stock the ranch range lease, and I have been picking up steers and heifers at the Cranbrook sales in the spring and feeding them for a few weeks prior to turnout May 1st to 15th, depending on grass growth. I still have one of our original stock, a black crossbred Angus-Shorthorn cow, who had her first calf March 12th, the night Mr. Benson, the Minister of Finance, brought down his White Paper, so I named him "Ben". His mother had him easily, but bawled piteously at this "thing" she had dropped! I had to rope him, from the hayloft above where "Ben" was lying in the snow filled entrance, and pull him into the barn. The mother was so upset when he moved that I didn't trust her enough to pick him up! By morning, all was well and by fall he had grown to a big 500 lb. calf.

I have three cows now; mostly I buy young stuff fall and spring, feed and range them and re-sell. I am not buying any this winter. Water is still a limiting factor in the winter. Here we have made extensive plans, 5,000 feet from the buildings we have a spring coming out of the hill, up a few hundred feet. We need height for pressure and do so hope we can get something done on this. It would be good to have a Pelton Wheel for electric generation at the site of the intake, and to lay cable and pipe in the same ditch. We'd be really set for anything then

Some Charolais cattle had a temporary home at the ranch this summer while their owner, an American, looked around for a spot to settle. He finally decided on the Okanogan. Charolais are not a breed I care for, being too coarse in bone. Phil Geiger, manager of The Swansea Ranch at Windermere, is importing one of the first Chiania bulls, an Italian breed. The huge animal weighs approximately 3,960 lbs. They have the smoothness that the Charolais do not have, as a rule. I wish them all the luck possible with their new project. Chianias, though the same colour as Charolais, are not as dominant and the progeny will probably take the familiar Hereford markings and colour more readily.

A real highlight in the close of the year's account was being able to enjoy ten days in the bright lights and whirl of Vancouver. Staying with dear old Prince George friends, the Lewall's, and having a real rest, free from all responsibilities (except that I was doing ranch business regarding the sale), was such a joy. Nellie and I went bird watching several Sundays, but our real thrill was during the visit to the Reifel Bird Refuge near Ladner, where we saw a rare bird, a Spotted

Red Shank. Believed blown off its migratory route by storms, it was keeping company with the shore bird of like habitats, the Dowitcher's. Being able to view so many species at close hand was really wonderful. While there, we saw Snow Geese, Trumpeter Swans, Whistling Swans, and many others, including the ten varieties of Canada Geese. Of interest to my readers, I think, would be the fact that George Reifel who has leased this area for 30 years to the B.C. Wild Fowl Association in the hope that they can make it self-supporting, is closely related to Lloyd's family, who were pioneer Windermere ranching folk.

Again, as always, so many grateful acknowledgements to the people who have assisted me so much by their interest and help in and on the place. As I close, we are busy getting wood in for the winter. The fireplace remains a real comfort and company on a cold winter night. The house is so beautifully insulated that it is no trick to keep warm with just wood. I love the smell of wood and am sure that it is the healthiest form of heat and certainly the cleanest, in spite of the dust.

To me, 1970 will always be remembered at Hidden Valley for the recognition finally granted me by the local range users. As a woman, I think (I felt anyway!), they thought it was a nuisance having to deal with a woman and that I probably would not be here long anyway! Now, they are willing to admit with a grin that I might be here another ten years!
A Very Merry Christmas and God bless you all.

Haying

Christmas 1971

I am starting this annual chore, always an enjoyable one, from the peaceful, quiet, ranch home of friends at Wasa, Betty and Bill Busch. They were in livestock transportation, and have sold their ranch to the B.C. Wild Life Service, but are still living there pending moving into Wasa. Nestled up under the Rocky Mountains, its situation is very similar to the Hidden Valley Ranch, which has been sold. The new owners, a group of Americans, now known as The Hidden Valley Christian Society, were sure before they even saw the ranch that it was the answer to their hopes and dreams. Frank Baynes, of Cranbrook, was the man that brought them up to see it. I met Frank years ago with Bob Megaw; it was good to be associated with him again in this momentous event.

Possession of the place was taken early in August and since then, things have really been happening at the ranch. The old log house, "The Homestead House", as they call it, has had such an overhauling that it is difficult to recall how uncared-for it had looked. It has a brand new green duroid roof, new chinking between the logs, wall boarded walls, a new floor, stacks of furniture and the old barrel heater from the basement installed. It recalled happy memories of helping Lloyd logging, when the lean-to kitchen, now a cow shelter, was full of hungry men, and when we taught English to the 14 German boys after supper at night when the dishes were done.

In the basement of the new frame house that Lloyd and I built, four bedrooms quickly took shape. The group ate meals altogether. It was, however, quickly obvious to me that with the best will in the world, these people, whom I would gladly have assisted in their new way of life, had to learn by themselves. There are so many of them, 18 at last count, not counting children. I am sure that they will manage.

This spring, early in May, Dorothy Hansen and I took the horse rack on my green half-ton GMC truck to Alberta to look for a Hereford bull for the range. We found a good young fellow, two years old, "Remittal Domino Mesa", at the Remittal Cattle Company home ranch at Olds. The name Remittal Cattle Company was a bit of a play on words, as people called

Lattimer owned it. They simply reversed their name. Carrol and wife, Jeannie, were so good to us. There is always a welcome there to a meal. This fine Western hospitality is getting very rare these days.

Dorothy, as always, looking for white shorthorns, asked Carrol if he had any for sale while we were being shown around his cowherd with their young calves. He said he had a young screwtail heifer that he would let go for meat price this fall at their annual fall sale. So, we three, Tug, Dorothy, and I went over to the sale on October 28th. Quite an experience! The day was complete with a lovely hot meal right in the barn. You could take it over and sit and watch the proceedings and eat, too. The Lattimer's really love their stock and it shows in the way they handle them in the ring.

When pulling into the motel at Olds the previous night, I forgot the height of the stock rack and knocked down the neon office sign in the carport. The Lattimer's were talking to the owner when the sign came crashing down, so, the next day, I was known as the lady who knocked the sign down!

We came home with "Nesnah Snowflake" in my new GMC truck. I was able to have a good stock rack built that matched the truck and has more than paid for itself with the cattle I have hauled safely and confidently. The green 1969 truck was a good one and gave me a real boost when I needed it, but it was starting to cost money. I was fortunate to meet Ted Swanson of Shaw's Truck Division in Calgary and he gave me a good deal, as my new truck was the last on the floor before the 1972 trucks were due. I was able to receive a rebate when the new ones came on the floor a few days later. This happened early in September and it was a real blessing during the fall round up.

July marked the passing of my mother. How I wish that she could have known that I had sold. She was so concerned about it. A quiet family funeral was held and her remains will be interred in Calgary. I have to try and see Mary, my sister, in the spring, to see the spot she chose near a creek. Mother loved a picnic by running water

August brought pressing work that could brook delay no longer, and that was getting my scattered cattle gathered up off the range. Half of these heifers were purebred Herefords, bought at the Cranbrook Auction this spring of Ray Van Steinburg's stock at Wycliffe. The rest were Tug Hansen's. His calves nearly always rate top prices at Cranbrook. These heifers did very well on the range, following a six-week pasture breeding period (from May 1st to June 16th) to a black, registered Aberdeen-Angus bull named "Tar Baby". They had an adventuresome time being hauled out of the range corral.

I still have a descendant of our original stock in a young heifer (this year's calf) that combines Shorthorn, Hereford, and Aberdeen-Angus blood and weighed out well in comparison to Fritz Maurer's exotic breed crosses. I was quite amused to find that one of his Limousin-cross calves weighed ten pounds less than my young "Inkspot", who was on the range all summer! Her weight was 530 lbs. Fritz bought her mother and wanted her, too. Her name was the result of one black spot on her all-white face.

For two months, from early September to late November, I was going out with other grazers when weather and their work would permit, to round-up. Firstly, I don't know how I could have managed without the kindness and hospitality of my friends, Tug and Dorothy Hansen of the Nesnah Ranch on Shuswap Creek. Their home was my base, even after I had purchased a small travel trailer, completely winterized. It was a real joy being able to load up my horse, "Kid", on the new GMC truck with stock rack to match and go riding for days if necessary, without having the responsibility of the ranch. I have been able to co-operate with the other range users this year, being near a telephone, in a way that has been impossible in the past, as often a decision to ride is made overnight. I am so thankful to be able to relate that all are safely gathered in. I waited at Wasa with some young-bred heifers, for the Cranbrook vet, Dr. Charlie Schornhorst, to pregnancy test them. They are all well on in calf, and were sold to The Three Sons Investments at Wasa.

What a beautiful place Ken Jennings has made of several homesteads along the east bank of the Kootenay River. Their huge twin silos on the hill overlooking the river are landmarks when traveling Highway 95 along Skookumchuk

Prairie. I was so pleased when Mr. Jennings came with his range rider, George Reveire, to see the heifers and made a deal right there. George told me they were as nice a bunch of heifers as he had seen for a long time, which was a nice compliment to a lady rancher!

Putting up the hay this year was fraught with potential disaster. July, our hay month, was extremely hot, ideal haying weather. I was gaily cutting it down, swath after swath of beautiful hay ready to bale the next day, and the man baling hay was having problems with the baler! It was awful to see all that beautiful hay burning up in the sun. In desperation, I went to see Ed Kirsch, our nearest neighbour, whom I felt sure was finished. Luckily, they were, so Ed came with his baler and loader. The last, a wonderful machine that picks up around fifty bales automatically and stacks them all at once on the 3 ton truck. Needless to say, I was very thankful when all was safely gathered in.

As you can well imagine, it is with a mixture of regret and relief that I leave the ranch. The new owners have kindly offered me lifetime tenancy, which only time will tell, whether I want to stay or visit under new management. I think there are just too many, but I shall for a few years anyway, take an active interest in the ranch.

The Tegart family had quite a reunion this fall, the occasion being Robert (Lloyd's brother) and Margaret's 50th wedding anniversary. Their sons and daughters and relatives from widely separated points came to salute them. It was held at the Invermere Community Centre. They received many lovely gifts and two lazy-boy chairs from their community friends.

Happy and Sharon Tegart have had an eventful year. They took over the management of the Lloyd Wilder Charolais herd at Fairmont. This was something new for them and one they approach with keen interest. As the summer progressed, it became apparent that they had succeeded in increasing the weight of this year's calves over last years. Happy and Sharon were busy preparing for a journey to take three animals to the Pacific National Exhibition, and they were busy putting finishing touches on them, when a large forest fire in the Dutch

Creek area came very close. Happy had to go out on a cat to help fight fire and the fire seemed to come closer. There was no telephone and poor Sharon was a very worried person. However, it was brought under control in time for them to get away. They were quite satisfied with their efforts and learned a great deal, too.

Managing to finish this letter seemed to be an impossible task this year, what with last minute details regarding ranch and stock, combined with the fact that the rough outline in my big pad never seemed to be handy! However, I am glad now that it was so, as I can give you the news of the "Thank you" and "In appreciation" gathering held on Sunday, December 5th from 3:00 to 5:00 pm. at The House O'Donald, a restaurant in Radium Hot Springs, owned and operated by Donald and Jessie Davis. Donald is Dorothy Hansen's brother and the two of them have been a real blessing to me. Their phone, a coffee and/or a meal, and above all, their welcoming smiles, have been a very real help these past four years. Getting this party arranged with Jessie, Sylvia, and Don was lots of fun. The many wonderful people who came seemed to thoroughly enjoy themselves. Lloyd would have really had himself a time and several voiced the thought that I had indeed done it in his memory. Certainly, only he could have made it a happier event for me.

My floor-length brown hostess gown, made by dear friend Lillian Detmer of Windermere, was much admired. Lillian, her husband, Sibbolt, and I basked in the compliments and it only took Lil one day to do it, after I made a flying trip from the ranch early December 3rd to pick up the material. It was trimmed at neck seam and on loose sleeves with gold sequins, and a lovely satin corsage loaned by Lil and Sibbolt, combined with gold slippers and evening bag completed my attire for this memorable occasion.

It is difficult to single out anyone of the over 100 who came. Many phoned, sickness and roads prevented some, but Tom Marr has to head the list. He faithfully came whenever he could, as he did when Lloyd was here, for over three years. Walter McKersie, who drove over 40 miles one way to help me run and maintain my forage harvester, that Lloyd had run mostly himself. They are a tremendous hay machine, saving so much time and work, but like any belt-driven machine, can be tricky and must be handled with care, especially near bush. Thanks to Walter, I survived some bad moments and learned enough to keep me going for four years. Very few were allowed on it after the first year, when a young man swung it around too fast near the bush. I gathered this, much later, from inspection and parts lying in the field at widely scattered points! Reno Goodwin, who was, until three years ago, the John Deere agent here, was always ready to come and assist with machinery problems. I cannot say how many times I thought of Lloyd.

One incident, I remember now with a smile, though it was no laughing matter at the time. The same enthusiastic young man who damaged the harvester, was setting up the tractor and water pump for irrigation at the bottom of the field and had the 2010 John Deere crawler with blade to level off a spot beside the creek. I was busy elsewhere and hours later he arrived to say, "It won't run!" In near despair, as the field was drying out fast, I went to discover that instead of just smoothing off what was already a good site, he had dug a hole and was trying to level off that! I'll never forget the position of the tractor and pump. Nothing could ever have worked.

Gene Berglund and friends, Ken and Ron, still going to High School in Kimberley, have helped for several years during haying and I have always enjoyed their company so much. It was so good to see them arrive for the "do" on Sunday at Radium. Leo Spiry came. How could I have managed without him with his always-ready smile and his chainsaw? It was good to see Larry Schable and friend, Ross, who volunteered this spring to paint the kitchen, bathroom, and entire living room, dining room ceiling for me, and went on from there to build a new corral, peeled posts and rails. It looked so nice, just in time for a good sale. Barbara Blakley, now at university in biology, was partner in the deal for the young bull. She was always eager to come out and help just to be there near the wilderness.

I still can't believe that I don't have all the responsibility of the ranch. When I was at my last grazing meeting, November 24th, I introduced the new Hidden Valley people to their fellow grazers and the Forestry men. Punk Pettigrew, of Hidden Valley, asked me how retirement felt. I said I couldn't believe it, as actually, although there is no more weight financially or otherwise, there are still lots of ends to tie up. There was still machinery to gather up, and measuring and settling on the hay, as neither hay nor cattle went with the place. The lifting of the financial burden was indeed wonderful

When I finally decide what to put in my trailer and take off for the south, it will only be for a few weeks, as I want to return and fix up the old "Corby Place". This beautiful 160-acre property is scheduled to be a provincial park eventually, in Lloyd's name. It is an ideal spot when completely fenced, to break out "Kid's' sister, "Melody", who is coming two next spring. My trailer will be parked by the spring where Lloyd and I had our tent when we were pruning the Christmas trees.

Just before leaving for Calgary and Vernon for Christmas, I checked with a rancher who was going to feed out my young bull, Mesa, for the spring bull sale to see how he was doing. He had come in off the range where he traveled well all summer, in rather poor condition. He was not responding to good pasture as he should, symptoms suggested "hardware" (cattle are prone to pick up wire nails, etc., and should all carry a magnet in their stomachs). When checked by Dr. Keith Marling on his monthly trip from Creston to Invermere, he agreed with this, inserted a magnet (hopefully) and prescribed combiotic every second day for ten days to two weeks.

The rancher was not satisfied when I phoned, so I decided to bring him over to Calgary to be checked at The Animal Clinic here, headed by Dr. Anderson, a great friend of Trevor Lloyd Jones, ex-principal of Guelph Veterinary College, whom we knew so well as children at The U5 Ranch in Edgewater. Dr. Birwash gave the young bull, Mesa, a clean bill of health. Dr. Marling's medication had done the trick and so, instead of going to the stockyard for slaughter, I took him back to his breeders at Olds for re-sale. It was very kind of Carrol to say that I could do this, but Dr. Birwash felt that he was probably being put on grain too fast at Windermere after having an upset stomach. It was good to see Laurie and her brothers and sisters. The school strike has them out of school just now, while their mother and father are away in the States with cattle, but that did not prevent Laurie from giving me a lovely chicken lunch while Bob unloaded "Mesa" and put him in a pen at home. Do hope he does well.

Before signing off, my thoughts being on the ranch, I feel that great things can be accomplished out there because they have the manpower that we lacked. They hope to cultivate the nearly 400 acres of arable land, and produce their own wheat for flour. They have their own stone-grinding machine. They plan to have vegetables, meat, and milk. I do hope this will prove possible.

After the weather being so dreadful in October, when we rode in 5" to 6" of snow, with the heavily laden trees dumping snow into our saddles and down our necks, it has been simply beautiful this past month. A few cool nights, but nothing to worry about with the cattle still browsing on pastures everywhere except out Hidden Valley way. Once snow comes there, it seldom leaves until April and May. This weather has been a real boon to stockmen not having to feed heavily until December.

My plans having been changed by my friend the bull, I have to return to the valley to take off the stock rack and put on the canopy, which is resting on Tug Hansen's old truck deck, then on to Vernon.

In the meantime, I am enjoying so much the hospitality of friends in Calgary, with not a care in the world at the moment. The war has caused me to lose contact with my foster son, Raju Injeti, in India.

So, until I see you, au revoir and God bless you always,

Christmas 1972

What a wandering life "Guard" and I have led since selling Hidden Valley Ranch last fall. I still, at time of writing, have not decided where I wish to put down roots. The East Kootenay country, the cattle auction sales at Cranbrook, and numerous ranching friends remain a constant pull to return there.

I have had such a varied existence in the past year, traveling from Vernon where I spent Christmas with the Megaw family, always a wonderful experience. Leaving January 4th via the Rutland-Rock Creek cut-off, the journey to Cranbrook was fraught with the possibility of slides.

Caring for Lillian and Sibbolt's family while Lil was in Calgary for a checkup was fun. I took Michael and Margaret to church with me. There was a huge drift to clear away and it drifted in again almost right away. A farmer clearing land a quarter of a mile away removed trees that had previously been a windbreak.

From Windermere, we journeyed via visits to the Ferguson's and other friends in Calgary to Airdrie where Sharon and Happy Tegart were busy caring for a large herd of Charolais cattle and a larger herd of commercial cattle. Willow Spring Farm is in a hollow, beautiful location, just a few miles northwest of Airdrie. These two versatile Tegarts are now with Adanac Wild-Life Films, located at Seebee in the beautiful, wild, mountain Kananaskis country.

When I visited the film company last February with them, we saw the grizzly bear, "Toklat". He is quite famous as the star of the film "Toklat." His pen mate, a black bear, allowed me to stroke his head through the wire. We discovered later that all the bears are de-fanged. His companions in the large film compound were a dozen or more coyotes, several pure timber wolves, some crossbred wolf dogs, a huge Kodiak brown bear, cougars, a leopard with a specially heated pen, elk, and deer. They all were seemingly quite happy in their surroundings. We were treated to the sight of a black bear out of his pen clowning with two attendants in the snow.

Getting back to Tug and Dorothy's Nesnah Ranch, I was just in time to discover that the bitter winter and deep snow was proving too much for "Kid" and "Melody". They were with Tug's horses, who remained fat and well on the Radium sloughs. I had to have them cared for by a ranger in Edgewater.

Leaving Airdrie, we headed back to the valley to dig the trailer out of the unusually heavy snow and ready it for the journey to the coast with Joyce, an old friend from nursing days at St. Eugene Hospital in Cranbrook. I was fortunate to find on arrival back in Windermere that Sibbolt had had a "cat" in the yard, to make a road down to the creek. So while there, he kindly arranged to have my home on wheels ploughed out.

Joyce and I outfitted the trailer from Tug Hansen's cabin, where my odds and ends are stored. After Joyce's son, John's, 24th birthday party on March 12th in Cranbrook, we left for the Trans-Canada and the Rogers Pass, wondering just how and when we would get through. It was quite an eventful two days. We stayed overnight at Donald, a few miles from Golden, amidst huge banks of snow, higher than the trailer, until we heard the okay from the highways department for the pass. Each day would see it open for a few hours, and then close again. We pulled out late in the afternoon, arrived at the Glacier Park east gate where a large lineup of huge trucks and other vehicles were being held up for slides. Every hour, for five hours, we were assured "just another hour"! So, we went to bed after having coffee and a sandwich in our cozy trailer. We felt so sorry for the many, but what could we do? At 1:30 a.m., we were told to proceed only a few miles to the summit, where we were held for the remainder of the night. At 7:00 a.m., everyone was urged on. We overslept and one of the highways' men rocked the trailer saying, "you are holding up the traffic"!! We two women broke a record, I am sure, in getting dressed that morning. We tumbled out of the trailer (no comb had been near our hair) to find not a vehicle in sight!! I could well imagine those guys having a good laugh behind the snow bank. Needless to say, we made tracks before another slide. The evidence was awe-inspiring. Huge cedars were torn up by the roots and splintered like matchsticks.

Reaching the coast went to Terry and Bub's lovely home at White Rock. Terry backed the trailer in beside a large dogwood tree near Elmhirst's trailer home. It was so peaceful and quiet there. It was there, as everywhere, a late spring, so that the ocean was not quite as attractive as usual. We enjoyed the beautiful show of flowers at the Bradner Flower Show where I nearly lost my precious camera, purchased in Prince George with the proceeds of boarding cats and dogs.

After Joyce left, I spent two lazy, satisfying months down there. Perhaps "Guard", because of the continued watchfulness necessary between him and Harvey, the McGillivary's watchdog, might have had reservations, but he could hardly complain, as he had such wonderful walks with Elmhirst, "Gretel", and I on the Old Semiahmoo Trail and other favorite walks.

I returned eastward via the Megaw's to cousin Eric's wedding to Cathy Lauer in Trail. Then I stayed at Abbotsford, enjoying catching up with cousin and goddaughter, Barbie Dalke's family news. It was there that I attended a service under canvas sponsored by the Pentecostal Church. It is good to see these Christian revivals and the way the young are responding.

Now, at time of writing, "Kid" and his sister, "Melody", are destined for the coast to stay in the care of Peter Tegart, whom I had not seen since he was nine years old until this fall when he was on a hunting trip with Jim and Doreen. Now in his 20's, Peter is a geologist with a large French mining concern. He lives in Vancouver and wants to know more about horses, never having had the opportunity. I do not want to have to worry about my nags until I know what I want to do, so in the meantime, this seems to be a happy arrangement. Peter will have to care for "Kid" and "Melody". Their home will be at Point Roberts with Peter's friend's horses.

I was interested to receive a newspaper clipping from Nellie Lewall about the Reifel Bird Refuge near Ladner, B.C. The Federal Wild Life Branch has purchased it as a bird sanctuary for the Canadian people.

Starting September 8th, I was back in harness again, caring for Jim and Doreen Tegart's Box 5 Ranch at Brisco while they took their hunting parties out in the mountains. As usual on a ranch, there was never a dull moment. In the first week, while starting to get the garden in with Doreen, Joe Scammell, from White Rock, arrived. She and I quickly got the vital vegetables in the root cellar, safe from frost, and then I took off for the Bugaboos.

I had two trips up there this fall, my first, which is rather ironic when we have lived so close for so long. It was a glorious fall day when Joe and I set off. We sat on the balcony at the lodge, soaking up the sunshine and heat reflected from the rough wood siding and had a delicious lunch brought to us by Lynne Seidler, Hans Gmoser's chief of the cooking department, and what pies! Lynne and Hans' partner joined us with a glass of wine. Facing us was the giant glacier with the famous Spires. It is a truly magnificent sight, the most breath taking in the mountains and well worth the 20-odd miles of gravel road to see.

The second trip, a week later, with John and Eileen Webb, was a bit "cagey" to say the least! Cecil Goodwin and his new Caterpillar D7 were busy making a new logging road across the face of a slide area and as it was wet and trying to snow, with a huge gray cloud hanging low, we though we had come to the end of the road! However, when I finally caught Cecil's attention (standing on a large rock at the edge of the bank and hoping Cecil would see me before he swiveled that big machine around), he renewed our hopes by saying that he would have it passable in half an hour. It was lunchtime and we had all the makings for lunch in the Volkswagen bus, so we decided to eat. Eileen had just had time to open two cans of soup when I said, "He's ready for us to go now!" So, go we did, with Eileen holding onto the opened cans of soup, over the rough road. John said that was the fastest 30 minutes he had ever experienced!

We ate the lunch on the lodge parking lot, watching the lower edge of the glacier and hoping that the cloud would lift. As Cecil had said to be back around 5:00 p.m. to get across the road-making, we did not dally too long, just long enough to look around the magnificent Swiss-style lodge, all done in rough, rustic lumber. Huge, thick boards and half logs are used for everything. A large black bell stands atop a giant slab of rock at the corner of the lodge and is attached by a cord to the balcony to call all and sundry from the slopes or wherever to meals. I find myself wishing I could ski into one of Lynne's meals.

Two young Tegarts, Susan and Clayton, were members of the first 4H Saddle Club organized in the Lake Windermere District this year. Susan is 11 and Clayton, at 10, is her nephew. Achievement Day, the last week in October, was a great day for all. Clayton had a pretty two-year old filly, newly broken this year and the two tried so hard to do well that the judge, the well-known Jim Wyatt of Appaloosa horse fame from High River, gave him the nod, saying "a green horse and a green boy", or really, he said "girl"! Poor Clayton, his hair was longer than the regular boy's cut, but not that long. He did not waste any time getting his mother busy with the scissors, much to Heidi's glee! The judge said that he hoped the next time he saw Clayton, he would know whether he was a boy or not!

The 4H banquet, held in the Invermere Community Centre, was a great success, almost double the number expected were there. Alan Wolfenden officiated in the awarding of the trophies after the two young 4H leaders, Anne Stephenson and Sonya Maurer, said brief welcoming speeches. Anne is dark and Sonya is fair, they made an attractive pair at the head table.

I was very interested in this event, as Winston Wolfenden and I participated in the beginnings of junior livestock work in the valley in the 30s. He and I won the East Kootenay finals held at Jaffray and if he had been able to go to the coast for the province-wide finals, we stood a very good chance of going to the Royal Winter Fair at Toronto, really something in those days. As it was, Ruth Peters went with me. When I look back on it now, I realize what a wonderful thing it was for her to go, as otherwise, the exciting journey and the sights and sounds of the many places we visited, would have been impossible for me.

November 7th marked a sale of interest to valley people, with the stock cow sale of dispersal herds. Bob Tegart's and Hans Hefti's formed the greatest numbers, nearly 200 head.

There were 400 head altogether that went through the ring that day. The cows making the highest prices that day were Hans', as they were bred to a half-Simmental bull, one of the "exotics". I was so glad for Hans and Rosa, a hardworking Swiss couple from Invermere, who had the good fortune to make a good sale for the place, which has a magnificent view overlooking Toby Creek, the Columbia River, and about three miles away, the Windermere Lake. They plan to be in Chilliwack this winter, but have retained 33 acres from the ranch in the event that they wish to return.

It was nearly the middle of November when I finally pulled away with the trailer from Shuswap Creek. The horses were supposed to be in Vancouver early in November! I arranged with Dr. Demetrick for a health inspection to cross the boarder into Point Roberts, and with Bob Primrose to trim their feet.

At the same time I am sitting here in Vernon trying to get this Christmas letter done. Being a one-finger typist is not conducive to getting very much accomplished quickly. I felt I should have the horses attended to here, probably a little more reasonable than at the coast. How I miss the canopy when it is off the truck for hauling stock, everything gets so damp. Randy Megaw enjoyed his brief ride on "Kid" last night after their inspection. Both horses have enjoyed wonderful care while with Bonnie Flintoff. "Kid" especially has put on weight.

The weather is still holding warm and lovely for this time of year, though it was decidedly winterish when I left the valley. Tug Hansen said I was going just "under the wire" and I think he was right. It was trying hard to snow when he pulled out with a load of cows for Cranbrook, shortly before I left.

Before I close, I must mention what a thrill it was to watch rancher-friend, Walter McKersie, his son, Brian, two helpers, and the Windermere vet, Dr. Slade, putting 500 cows through the chutes in one day for pregnancy testing. I think that must have established a record for the valley. Walter is operating The Elkhorn-Alpine spreads together with his and Betty's larger Thunder Hill Ranch. Quite an undertaking and I wish the McKersies all the best. I enjoyed a short overnight visit with Bertha McKersie, Walter's mother, who lost her husband not long ago. I was glad to know that she will be visiting with a sister this winter, back on the prairie.

There was one sale that I feel will be remembered in years to come. It was held in Edgewood, early in November and represented 20 years of work with a "closed herd" policy used under the supervision of Dr. Roy Berg, well-known animal geneticist, a cross between the dun Highland cattle and the milking shorthorn. They are bred for mountain snow areas. After a glance at the animals Winston Wolfenden chose and brought home, I am glad I did not go. I know I would be tempted and have no home for them! I must also mention my yearling black white face heifer, "Inkspot", staying with Tug and Dorothy on The Nesnah Ranch. She has grown and is fat and sassy to go into the winter with their cattle, all of which come home November 1st from summer range across the Columbia River.

Christmas tree care on the Olde Corby Place has been arranged with Ron Ede, and I want to get the place fenced come spring, if possible, as cattle are getting in from the mountain side and I am afraid of damage in the spring from trampling hooves.

Knowing that I miss the solitude and peace of the ranch, a dear friend sent the following, with which I close....

"We think of silence too much as the hush which results when we have managed to get rid of some particular noise. It would be better to think of it as something in its own right, as something which noise violates."

--- Dom Hubert Van Zellar

Merry Christmas all.

Christmas 1974

The season's best to all. This year was either too short, or I tried to do too much, but it just flew. Talking about moving fast made me think of a delightful episode which occurred at Dawson Creek in August while visiting with dear friend, Alma Henderson. She and I had gone out to see the Thompsons, friends of hers at Rolla, a wee village just out of Dawson Creek where Alma and Gus had homesteaded and where Walter, their son, still lives and farms with his wife and family. Roy Thomson, it turned out, was a keen horseman who not only raises quarter horses, but was also the proud owner of a spanking team of chestnut Arab-Percherons. A ride in Roy's dandy four-wheel homemade buggy was one of the highlights of the year for me. In fact, I was fully intending to head this letter, "The Horses That Looked Both Ways"!!

The Thomson's place is on a corner of a fairly busy country crossroad and when we drove out, Roy pulled them up at this crossing and told them to look up the road, which, believe it or not, they did, each one looking his and her way. Bell and Donnell, five and seven year-old brother and sister, gave us a grand fast ride and, joy of joys, on the return, Roy handed me the lines, which to me, was both a thrill and a compliment. It has been a good many years since I held the lines over a good pair of horses. When we came back to the crossing near home, I pulled them up and repeated what Roy had said, not really believing that they would look. In the knowingly beautiful way that only a horse can look, they did, each one, look up the road before being given the go-ahead. Roy was right on when he said, "You didn't believe they would, did you?"

To go back to earlier in the year, after an always-wonderful Christmas with the Megaws in Vernon, I set forth with the trailer for Point Roberts, where I should have been in late September! I'm sure Peter and John had just about written me off! However, my charges, eight or nine horses, including two that I raised, were being well cared for, which left me free to handle and train my little half-Arab mare for the saddle.

Before starting on "Melody", quite to my surprise, I found myself chatelaine of a lovely old three-bedroom summer cottage for the remainder of the winter. It was from there that I was able to talk to "Melody" every day and get to know her again. She was quick to learn and it was no time, considering the really small time I spent on her, before I was riding her, which we both enjoyed as we rode off the 60 acres in the surrounding country. "Melody" was bred to "Sultan", a registered Arab, and is now expecting her first foal in May.

Early in June, I had the trailer on the Olde Corby Place and what a beautiful spot it is. The fences need doing badly, as the wire and posts are all down. I spent a few weeks there in glorious weather with a bear and "Guard" for company. Regretfully, due to previous commitments, I had to leave the little bit of paradise that Lloyd left me. It's a very good thing that I do have a few things I have to do, or I'd go nowhere!

Going up to Prince George, the first time since leaving there in 1960s, I was able for the first time in my life to see the famous Jasper Highway in the summer. I stopped at the Columbia Icefields and watched the snowmobiles crawling with their loads of tourists over its vast white surface. The last time I saw a snowmobile was when I worked at Sunshine Ski Camp many years ago, and the snowmobile was our only transport into town. Clint, the driver, used to work at the Icefield in the summer. I wonder where he is now?

While in Prince George, home sitting for friends, Erla (a niece and her three children), a friend and I spent a few rewarding hours at Barkerville, which has a special meaning for Lloyd's branch of the Tegart family, as his mother, Mary Brown, was born, raised, and married there. Mary's sister, Lottie, was really part of the history of Barkerville. Lottie owned and operated the well known Kelly Hotel and store. Many a hard-luck miner had cause to be grateful for the grubstakes from the Kelly store. George Kelly, Lottie's son, started the museum, which was eventually taken over when the Social Credit government, under W.A.C. Bennett, commenced restoring British Columbia's historic old places.

Later, friends Tug (Trygvie) and Dorothy Hanson, from the valley, were on Lightning Creek in the Barkerville area and I spent a lot of time hunkered down, panning for gold. We all managed to find some, which Dorothy carefully put in little plastic bottles and labeled. At a later date Wild Horse Creek, near Fort Steele, saw us busy again, and we found colour there too, and the country was so beautiful in the fall colours.

From Prince George, early in August, "Guard," and I took off for the Peace River country, Dawson Creek particularly, to see Alma Henderson. Alma and Gus became friends when Lloyd and I joined in the 1957-58 campaign to put John Diefenbaker in Ottawa. Gus was a Conservative candidate for the huge riding of Prince George – Peace River, the largest in Canada, I believe. It was a very good thing for us that Gus was in Ottawa, as our Veteran's Land Act loan, which had been approved, was denied. They thought we couldn't do it, so far from all services, we discovered later. When Gus heard we had nearly 80 acres ploughed and no money for seed, things started to move! Later, far from denying us, our V.L.A. friends offered us a second loan.

While with Alma, we went on a camping trip over to Fairview, where I knew there was a young Tegart in bees. I had heard about Dave and Gwen from Dave's mother in Richmond, B.C. Mary was so proud of those two and no wonder. Ten years ago, at the age of 19, Dave left home for the Peace River country with $100.00. Last year, he and his wife, Gwen, grossed $250,000 with their bees. Their success can be attributed to their courage and determination when, for three winters, they took work way up north on runways and in logging camps to earn the best possible money in order to finance the bee venture. They have a lovely spot on a knoll, facing south, just out of Fairview, Alberta and are in the process of building themselves a new home.

Before leaving Dave, Gwen, Charlotte, two years, and Daniel, seven months (August 1974), I must tell you that they, like all farmers, depend so much on the weather. If the weather is bad, the bees won't work, they eat the honey instead! In the fall, especially, is a critical time; the day comes when they must be gassed. One hive will eat two pounds of honey a day and when you have 500 hives!! They go down to California in the spring, holidaying on the way down, non-stop coming home, bringing the new bees.

November marked a very special event in Canadian rodeo circles. The first ever Canadian rodeo finals were held in Edmonton in conjunction with the Farm Fair and Exhibition. I was invited to join Happy, Sharon, and their newly adopted son, Rob, for the event. I took in the Simmental cattle sale and purchased a valuable Simmental heifer for Hap and Sharon.

The end of November marked my debut into the mink pelting business. Fred and Dollie Yerbury were selling out their mink ranch and I figured it would be quite an experience. It was. I was glad that I was still fit from ranch work, as it was hard work. With an eleven person crew we had to prepare every pelt for sale. We worked a nine hour day every day from Nov. 20 – Dec. 5. Fred Senior and Fred Junior did the skinning, Kay, Sherry, and Flo fleshed them, Nina and Mary shaped them, and Marge and I put them on boards. After than they were drummed, racked and sanded. Dollie Yersbury oversaw everything. After the pelts were finally finished and everything at the ranch was cleaned up, Fred took us all out to dinner and December 7th found me settled in at the coast. It was lovely to see family and friends again.

Peter and Jarmila Tegart had a daughter, Alexandra, born August 22nd. Peter came down from the Yukon where he was working for the event. She is a very beautiful young girl.

There remains only to say so long for 1974. Wishing you all the very best for 1975. Hopefully, I set off for warmer climes, Arizona, after the New Year, for a couple of months, anyway.

With my love to all,

"Guard" joins me with a tail-wag or two.

Christmas 1975

Something that has been buzzing around in my head for a long time is the idea of a "round-robin" letter of family news and views from as many of you as would care to join in the fun. How do you think it would go?

Many of the younger members, while not wishing to become actively involved are still very interested in knowing about their roots. I hope to spend next summer with Alice Green, 80 years young, at Bond Head, Ontario, who has such a lot of family history in her four huge scrapbooks, and what isn't in them, is in her head. Together, perhaps we can put a "start" together.

Early last spring, in Vancouver, B.C., I babysat six-month old Alexandra for Peter and Jarmila Tegart while they took four days off, for a business holiday for Peter to Calgary. Guess it was cold there, as they both returned convinced that was no place to live! I love the coast, too.

Sherry Newcomen (nee Tegart), James Sinclair Tegart's daughter, her husband, Henry, and three children are presently living in Vancouver, and I visited with them. We even took Guard up for the night to their apartment! Henry is a journeyman electrician, doing very well, won them both a ten-day holiday in Paris recently (October).

I saw Larry and Heidi, Jim Tegart's son and daughter-in-law, at Harrogate, B.C. on their Tangus Ranch. They were originally in Aberdeen Angus, now in Charolais purebreds. Larry drives a "cat", doing roadwork on contract. Far less nerve wracking than running your own outfit (logging) under N.D.P. All forest work was at a standstill this year in B.C. Many private contractors were forced out of business.

While with them, I thoroughly enjoyed going to the 4H banquet and saw Shilo, their second son, receive his awards. Lorraine and Elwood Goodwin were there and their son, Douglas, had awards, too. Lorraine (nee Tegart) is Janice Schneider's older sister. Lorraine and Elwood have this year moved into their lovely new home on their land up above Edgewater.

I saw Jim and Doreen Tegart at their Box T Ranch, Brisco, B.C. for a little while. They are always busy and often not home. They still have their hunting and guiding outfit and go up into the mountains every fall with their pack outfit, horses, diamond hitches, etc. The hunters are mostly American.

Jim is a younger brother of my husband, Lloyd, who was the eldest in a family of 13 (12 lived), children of Arthur Henry and Mary Louise. Mary was born and raised at Barkerville, B.C. Her family was well known in that famous old gold rush town, which is preserved as a historical site and is being beautifully restored. Well worth going to see.

Hanen Interests of Calgary and the neighbouring Elkhorn ranch now own the Alpine Ranch at Windermere. It was at the Alpine Ranch that Arthur and Mary raised their family, from whom all the Columbia Valley Tegarts are descended. George, next to Bob (died 1960) owned the U5 Ranch at Edgewater. His widow, Lillian, and son, Denis, and daughter-in-law, Rose Marie, live there today. Janice and husband, Ben, and family have land and a lovely home on the north end of the U5 Ranch. Ben is with the Kootenay National Park at Radium Hot Springs.

I have heard from Margaret Leach of Alliston, and Alice Green, with news of the Ontario clan. I'm afraid all mail will be late this year. Dear Polly, from Austin, has a great care with hubby, Preston, (who has Parkinson's disease) and is a faithful writer. I never think of Polly and the Texas family without remembering Phil and his question, "Is Guard a good watch dog?" When I asked him if he wanted to test him, I think he wondered what he had gotten into! I wondered, too, as Guard had his two half-hour training periods in January, and here we were in the middle of April. Anyway, Guard "rose" to the occasion literally by grabbing Phil's arm, on command, in mid air. I assured Phil that all would be well if he stood still, which he did. Guard has a wonderfully light mouth and is always leading me around by holding my arm, especially when he wants something, to go out mostly.

I made two trips out to Irricana, Alberta, 40 miles northeast of Calgary. One in September for a week and later in

November, I took my Arab mare and foal over there to Happy and Sharon Tegart. They are running a very smart spread, boarding and fitting cattle, which includes clipping and readying cattle for show. All cattle dealt with are of the large exotic breeds. Charolais from Dundas Farm in Prince Edward Island form the majority of these boarders.

This year has been unusual for me. A new avenue of interest has opened up, animal babysitting, which I enjoy very much. How often, in the past, Lloyd and I would have given anything almost for someone to come and care for our animals so we could get away, even for ten days or two weeks. Farmers and ranchers just cannot get away. City and urban dwellers, I am sure, do not realize how tied farming folk are. So, I am enjoying this new way of life. It is not a tight schedule, but satisfying and brings in a little money, always welcome.

Often, I wonder what I am doing with no base, but if I had one, I couldn't travel and be free to go anytime. So, for the time being, I shall enjoy my present way of life.

I had hoped to head south again, but I may be needed and in March, I assist friends in Radium. Presently, I am caring for pets of Evie and Per Groland, dear friends of Prince George days, who are in Norway for a month over Christmas. Christmas will be with Tug and Dorothy up at Radium and my cousin Dorothy at Edgewater.

May God bless you and yours always.

Christmas 1976

Each year, when time comes to set my pen to paper for the annual Christmas letter, memory takes me back to our first years on The Hidden Valley Ranch. Lloyd had owned it since the fall of 1941, he was busy ploughing with horses, had no radio, and did not know about Pearl Harbour until the weather sent him into town, late in December. Two decades later when Lloyd and I were living on the ranch he always enjoyed my Christmas letters.

Lloyd was interested and pleased with the description of what we had accomplished that year. Our friends of The Veteran's Land Act told us that our letter was like a breath of fresh air in the offices at Kelowna and Ottawa. I can still see the grin that spread over Lloyd's face when I read him the letter from the Veteran's office. So every year, it was a pleasant task, often done during a snowstorm when we were housebound anyway. I remember one year we were weaning and the bawls of cows and calves made concentration a might difficult.

I miss the routine and varied activities of ranch life very much, even after five years of supposed retirement. The 160 acres that Lloyd bought back in the '30s has been such a joy to me. This spring, it was the scene of some activity as it was badly in need of fencing. In some spots, a new stretch of wire was needed; in others, it meant picking up the old wire, which was still in excellent condition.

Early in May, I was thrilled to see Elliot Trueman burst over the horizon one evening as I sat in the trailer watching the coyotes weave in and out amongst the grazing cattle. Elliot and his brother, Jim, had driven up from Vancouver to assist and between us, with Betty Busch's help, we put up the north end quarter mile of fence.

Since then, with the help of other friends and my retired sister, Mary, we have made good progress on the east mile. This has been rather a slow process, as it has meant finding and picking up three strands of wire, which has been down for 30-odd years, overgrown with juniper, willow, and young fir trees, many of which had to be cut, unfortunately, it has been a satisfactory operation. I love being out in the bush and put in many happy hours this summer.

I also spent many hours schooling my young Arab, "Rainbow". Elliott and Jim helped me get started on a pasture for him, adjoining the old barn, before they had to leave for the bright lights again. "Rainbow", though only a yearling, changed quickly from a tendency to be wild into a typical people-loving Arab. He loved his training periods. He was also initiated into the business of being tethered, always a useful thing to know.

I had always longed to train a horse along English equitation lines and Sharon Tegart had loaned me a good book on this, so "Rainbow" and I learned together. I found he was so quick to pick up his teaching that I had to really know what I was doing and keep moving ahead, as he tended to become bored. Since early August, he has been running with the six Hansen horses in their large 1100-acre pasture across the Columbia River from Radium Hot Springs. There, he learned to swim the channel with the others (we had high water until quite late, with all the extra rainfall). I had a grandstand view one evening as the horses crossed the channel. It was a real thrill for me to watch and see how my youngster handled himself with all those veterans. I fully expected to see him fearfully bringing up the rear. Not so. He and one of the mares were last, and he went ahead of her. All the traveling they do from the high country bunch grass down to the sloughs has straightened his feet and legs out. He tended to toe-out a little with his hind feet. It is also good for his lung and heart development. Dreamer me, thought someday, he might do cross-country and/or jumping. He has a quarter thoroughbred blood from his maternal grandmother, which gives him more height and scale than a purebred Arab usually has. He was well over 14 hands as a yearling.

August saw Dorothy, Tug, and me putting up the logs on their new home across the river at Radium. The logs were all lathed 7½ inch logs, the longest being 21 feet. Dorothy and I were the lead oxen, our yoke, a short 2 x 4 under the end of the log, with Tug taking the full weight of the other end, away we went up the good wide ramp Tug had made. When one phase was finished, it was on with the roof. Dorothy and I were not the least bit sorry to see the roof finished. Looking down into space, even if it was only 20 feet or so, was not for us!

My wee trailer, my home on wheels in the good weather, has seen a lot of use this year. It sat in the shade of the barn, so well concealed from view that several people came in and thought I had pulled out. The Corby Place was a very happy home for "Rainbow", "Guard", and me for several months. With "Rainbow" tethered out around the trailer, he often put his nose in the door and started trying to run off with my towels hanging by the door. It would have become a regular game if I had encouraged it!

Coyotes were a common sight amongst the grazing Elkhorn cattle on the flat. I have never seen so many. The local ranchers are plagued with them. They kill cats, chickens, and dogs. Their favorite strategy with dogs is to have one coyote lure the dog into nearby bush, and then they gang up on him. Fortunately, most dogs are instinctively aware of what will happen. It was comical to watch the nonchalant way the coyotes would trot in amongst the cows and calves, until one cow would decide to put the run on him and off he'd go. On a neighboring ranch, where no one is presently living, coyotes have raised a litter of coyote-dog crossbred pups. These are far worse from the ranchers' point of view, as they are much bolder. A local trapper has caught most of them, but one pup is too wise. He digs and scratches around the trap until it is tripped, then he enjoys the bait. Only lead will stop that fellow.

This winter, I am staying with my friends, the Hansen's, at Radium, keeping an eye on "Rainbow", helping where I can, and trying to get going on the Tegart history, also an account of my family, although there is not the same urgency there, as it is all fairly well documented in England.

For the Tegarts, a rather wonderful thing happened from a genealogical point of view this last summer. Murray Mitchell, has this year been up to the valley from his home in Abbotsford, at the coast. Though their time was short, they were given a tour by Robert Walker Tegart of The Alpine Ranch area, where all the B.C. and Alberta Tegarts from the Arthur Henry line originated. Bob owned The Alpine Ranch for many years. He and Margaret raised their family of eight children there. After Bob's tour, Murray and Betty invited me to dinner, after which we spent a happy evening, during which I was able to find out a great deal more on the family.

Henry and Sherry Newcomen and family have returned to their home and electrical business in Invermere, on Lake Windermere. June, Sherry's sister, also daughter of Jim Tegart, and her husband, Pete, are spending the winter out on her father's hunting territory, trapping. Peter and Jarmila Tegart and wee daughter, Alexandra, have recently moved into their first home, not an apartment, in North Vancouver. I am so glad for them. Living in apartments can be trying for a young couple with a child. Ali won't know what to do with herself with so much room and a large garden, too. Happy and Sharon, on their half section at Irricana, are doing well, very well with the boarding and fitting cattle, for which they are building themselves quite a name.

Now, the first week in December, Hap is away on the show circuit, and Sharon keeps the ball rolling at home. With upwards of 150-200 head of stock on hand, with their various needs met, it is a responsible undertaking. Their young son, Robbie, three year-old dynamo, will soon be a big help to them. Last summer, he showed his pony and rode in a parade. He is quite a help opening and closing gates, though he often, childlike, fails to see the need for opening and closing quickly!

Happy just arrived back from Regina with the heartening news that purebred cattle prices are holding up well. All breeds, including the British breeds, and new breeds like Chianinas, are doing well. They are going to Canadian buyers with a view to going south eventually. One well-known livestock man is buying up good big cows now, while the general market is so poor, the little man is being forced out of business.

Coming out to Calgary the end of November, I came via Golden and visited with Kathy Braisher, near Parson. I had not seen her since the year I sold The Hidden Valley Ranch, in 1971. Her father, Winston Wolfenden, was in Junior Livestock judging with me back in the '30's. Dugan, her husband, is doing great things in the valley, clearing land. This year, he had a good contract with the government, developing water resources.

No journey through Golden or Calgary is complete without a visit to the Grolands who we knew from our Prince George days. The same hold with trips to the Okanogan and visits with the Megaws. The trans Canada highway was in excellent condition, bare and dry, like driving in the summer. My sister, Mary, is now retired from her government position, and is living in a large mobile home on our cousins' (Paddy and Dorothy) property at Edgewater. Aunt Barbara, my mother's sister, who was with Dorothy, has recently been admitted to a new senior citizen's home in Kimberley, a two-hour drive from Radium. The home feels that the traveling at Christmas time is not in their best interests, which we all appreciate, though she will be missed.

Talking to Robert and Dorothy Woodall (Lloyd's eldest) for their news, I found that far from tomatoes, they find themselves producing potted flowers and baskets by the thousands at Priddis, near Calgary, for The Bay and Simpson Sears, mainly. This all developed from what was originally a family affair and grew from that small beginning. Robert told me that they had been trying various methods, purely theory, some of which had proved quite successful, so much so, that people have been coming to see and discuss these methods, with a view to using these ideas. Robert said that the turnover for this past year was in the $25,000 bracket and that next year, 1977, they hope to see this doubled. They have 15,000 square feet under fiberglass, using two million B.T.U.s of gas-generated heat. All this keeps family and friends "on the bit". Robert is not keeping too well, but spends little time thinking about it.

This closes my good wishes to all. May the Lord bless you and keep you always.

Christmas 1977

What a grand snowfall we have just had, the skiers dream. The acres of tall fir trees surrounding the house are loaded with snow, and just beautiful in the bright sunshine.

It is wonderful being here at the "Nesna Ranch" west of Radium. I am fortunate to be able to join in and be a part of this loving family. I enjoy the hustle and bustle of a family. It reminds me so much of our "Hidden Valley Ranch" days with many of the same joys and challenges. We are living under pioneer road conditions and as yet, several days after the snowfall, there is no sign of the snowplough. The government are pretty good, considering their problems.

Dorothy Hansen, co-owner of the "Nesnah Ranch", and I took the children to the Disney show in Invermere, ten miles away, on Saturday following the snow and only the main roads were ploughed. There were people walking happily everywhere in town. The drivers were going slowly, enjoying the confusion.

. We have been dragging snow with the bottom of the truck, as we break trail out to the railroad. It is a distance of about a mile and "Guard loves to run gaily alongside on his daily jog. What with packing water from either town or the river until the past week and bringing in wood for the fireplace and heater, life stays busy. The children have to be driven across the river to school and home again and also to music lessons etc.

Tug (Trygvie) Hansen has been a very busy and often frustrated man as he has been ironing out the various wrinkles from the electric and water systems. What a joy it was to eventually see that precious liquid coming out of the taps, and especially into the toilet. It was not by any means a smooth process. It really bought back memories of Lloyd an I at the Hidden Valley Ranch.

We had such a struggle getting the septic and water lines dug and a pressure pump in the newly cribbed well after the old cribbing had given way. Vandalism had visited the ranch in spring of 1962. When we returned from Calgary where we had spent a happy winter in Lloyd's daughter and son-in-law's old home by the Bow River, the 24-foot galvanized pipe to the water had disappeared from the well. From the tracks, Lloyd judged it had been taken only a few days before our return. It was a great blow to Lloyd. It was as much the thought that anyone would do that to him, as the financial loss, which was considerable to us at that time.

My dear friends the Hansons had less water troubles, as they were fortunate to dig a spring not far from the house so there is an ample supply of water. It was not so easy obtaining power to the ranch. It was quite a fight to obtain their fair share of power. There was a program called Rural Electrification Assistance, which should have smoothed things out. Due to lack of cooperation from Revelstoke sawmills, Hydro and Forestry the Hansens were forced after eighteen months of futile negotiations, to close and barricade the road, which runs through their property and for which, they have received no remuneration for many years use. Tug wanted nothing to do with the barricade, but Dorothy and I stood our ground. The first twenty-four hours of manned closure was not the sort of thing one want to do. There were many who tried to run the gauntlet, but were turned back. We had family at both ends. "Guard" did his bit when some young fellows thought they were going to force the issue in the early hours of the morning.

There was over four months of closure. It was felt that if the barricade didn't stand that even with assurances that power would be delivered within 5-6 months, that the wait would likely be two years. With the surveyors actually on the ground now, in the snow, we feel confident that power will be here by spring anyway. It is a great satisfaction after all of the worry and the phone calls to Victoria.

Early in March "Guard" and I set off for Prince George to visit with friends, some new, some old faithful ones. We enjoyed our time with the Baldwins. Dear friends from Prince George days, Bunnie and Nellie Lewall, had their golden wedding anniversary early in October. I don't realize it was their fiftieth, or wild horses couldn't have kept me away. I was so sorry to miss this. Bunnie was the chief survey engineer in charge of construction of the Pacific Great Eastern Railway from Prince George north to Dawson Creek and Fort St. John. We met Bunnie and Nellie because of a washing machine. It developed into a wonderful friendship. From Prince George I went on down to the coast after visiting various Tegarts on the way down.

My sister Joan was out from Ontario in April. A surprise to us all. A wonderful one to me as I have seen very little of her since her school days before the war. I was in the Fraser Valley when I heard she was at my cousins in Edgewater with my sister Mary. I was due for a horse-sitting job at Cloverdale, but I made a quick return to the valley to be with them. Joan is not well, which troubled me. My vital kid sister not well! I couldn't believe it. She did enjoy seeing all of the old familiar haunts again, and was certainly more relaxed when she went home. Since her visit, I am relieved to know that she is in good hands. She refers to her three doctors as "my battery".

I returned to Cloverdale to do my horse sitting. Dear old "Kid", my eleven-year-old Anglo-Arab lives with other equine friends in a happy home where he is loved and used. It is always a pain to part with beloved animals, but the parting is easier when you know they have a good home. I enjoy visiting "Kid" in his Cloverdale home. I wended my way home slowly visiting friends and family in Abbotsford, South Slocan and Moyie Lake.

A wonderful visit was had here in the valley with Trevor and Edgar. Trevor is an old friend from U5 days in the late 1920s and Edgar was a classmate who also became a good friend. It was lovely to see both men and their wives.

This was an extra special year for the Tegart clan. The James Tegarts of Brisco hosted the first Tegart Reunion. After a great deal of work by five of Lloyd's nieces, the weekend of July 30/31 saw the meeting of over four hundred Tegarts at the Edgewater Campground. They came from: Houston and Austin Texas; Portland, Oregon; Halifax, Nova Scotia; Brome, Quebec; Ontario (where the Canadian Tegart story began), and the prairies. Of course there were several from the valley alone.

The highlight of the reunion for me was the meeting of the two oldest members of the Tegart family. Polly and Alice, both in their eighties, met for the first time at Calgary where they had traveled alone by air. Getting those two dear souls together was a very real joy to me. One of Lloyd's nieces had offered to put them up for me, and as she is a Tegart it was grand for them both to catch up on the family story. The Vancouver Sun had the reunion written up, with special mention on the front page in their Focus column.

I was disappointed not to be able to show them around, but due to the threatened air controller's strike, they had to take the first available plane out of Ontario, where Polly visited kinfolk. Polly was shielded from the knowledge of her 99-year-old sister Essie passing away in Lyle, Texas at the time of the reunion. Polly wrote that Essie went in her sleep. I would have enjoyed showing Polly and Alice The Olde Corby Place and if the weather had been good I could have had them stay in my trailer for a few days.

My three year old "Rainbow" has been a joy to me. He spent two months with me at the buildings learning his manners with the saddle, the bit, the works except for riding. He won't get much riding until his fourth year if he is to be pointing at jumping. I was on him, and he went around the corral beautifully, obeying the commands that I had trained him from the ground. Next year, I'll have some one lead him with me in the saddle, just so he knows. He is so quick to learn it is a joy to work with him. "Rainbow" leads a happy life with the Hansen's six horses in their huge pasture and on the sloughs. Occasionally they are on the range in the hunting season, when the hunters leave gates open. At least they get some new feeding areas, which is good for them.

Looking out of the window at all this beautiful, softly falling snow, and listening to the muted sound of the diesel generator, giving us light and power, watching for the cattle to wade through the deep snow for their daily feed, from their beds deep in the bush, I close this narrative.

With love to all

May our dear Lord guide and protect you always.

Christmas 1988

With snow on the ground, all the horses with their furry winter coats, and the church concerts, the festive season is here again, and I am all behind on my cards, which never go out without quite a few words about my doings, in response to all the wonderful news I receive.

I went over to England in June for the wedding of a young cousin. Tina married Chris Snell, a young helicopter pilot in Exebridge, Somerset, June 17th, in a little local stone church at Brushford. I traveled around in England visiting an Air Force friend in Lancashire, and a Christian Israel friend in Birmingham. Then I went back to Somerset and Devon to my father's home, a lovely sheep farm, "Holwell Barton" and my cousin's large farm home in Somerset, "Riphay Barton", a friend in Wiltshire. I returned to London where John and Hermione Skrine welcomed me both coming and going.

John was a real blessing to me on the ranch in 1971, when I sold the Hidden Valley Ranch. He did all the errands in my old VW truck and made all my phone calls. He was very responsible for being only 17 years old. Good help is so necessary at such a time, when one is 20 miles from the nearest phone and post office over a narrow mountain road.

I returned home to a forest of weeds waist high. I shall not take a trip again at that time of year!!

A busy summer followed. Kind neighbors put up my hay, which was a real blessing. Quite a sight! Nineteen huge round bales (approximately 1500 lbs. each) in my small hayfield. A young friend did irrigation while I was away. Beautiful fall weather signaled the hunting season. I am always glad when it is over, as my gate has to be locked. Friends use my place (with keys) to hunt the mountainside, above me, for deer and elk.

My equine friends make the place lively with their antics, as they have 160 acres in which to roam. I do enjoy watching them from my kitchen window. In fact, without the animals, the place would be too quiet. It is a horse paradise. Plenty of open areas to run and a spring a half mile up the hill. Bandit, my black cat, comes tearing from the barn when I come home. Until a few weeks ago, there were two furry fellows, Smokey, my Siamese, too. They meet me often way down the road, a quarter mile from the cabin. My real puss cat pal, Smokey, met his fate with either an owl or a coyote. I really miss him. He was special. Am on the lookout for another Siamese, as they really are characters.

So now I must close, listening to the warm, cozy sound of the wood-burning range in my wee log cabin.

Later - I did not close, nor proceed with this, as I fell on cement and badly damaged my old weak knee. That was five days ago, December 16th. My place is strewn with cards and letters untouched since then, so I beg your forgiveness, as I know replies, etc. will not be away before the New Year. I have not even got the regular cards away, only the overseas and a few long distance Canadian ones. "Dusty", my cross-Samoyed-coyote bitch, watches anxiously, as I hop around on crutches and faithfully picks up anything I drop. Friends keep an eye on me, so all is well. Snow is falling, but not enough. Wonder if we will ever get a good old-fashioned heavy fall of a foot, anyway! We surely need it. Each summer is getting drier and drier.

May the rich blessings of this precious season, commemorating Our Savior's Birth, be with you now and always.

Christmas 1989

Cool weather is a great reminder of the season. Water is freezing in the irrigation ditch. The horses, newly let into the hayfield for the winter after tearing around full gallop, tails in the air, are full and thirsty, so they impatiently paw their way through the thin covering of ice and stand drinking, while swishing lumps of ice away with their lips.

I was out on a lonely mountain road not far from our old "Hidden Valley Ranch" a few days ago to see a friend and his huge machine doing range seeding work for cattle grazing. His wife and young son are also camping with him. While with them, they told me what they knew about the huge German Shepherd dog that had adopted them. They believed he was abandoned, as he anxiously searched every vehicle, especially trucks, that drove by, hunters mostly. It breaks my heart to see dogs and cats deserted, especially at this time of year. They are so dependent on us and all it takes to be merciful is a bullet, clean and quick, rather than know they will suffer from hunger and the pain of knowing their loved ones have deserted them. I wrote a letter to the editor of our local paper about this.

My Christmas letter has to be done fairly early for overseas mail. A good thing too, as I just cannot get enthused to collect Christmas thoughts so early. I leave that to the commercial marts!

The woodpile is all ready for winter's onslaught. I went to Calgary in early October for my annual load of coal. Three-quarters of a ton! My half-ton was loaded. I also got groceries from the Co-op that has met my needs so well for a number of years. I came home in a blizzard; went to Alberta through one, too, as I took a load of fence posts for friends moving to Black Diamond with their horses. These friends, and another couple, will be sadly missed next year for our annual small horse show, as they, being good friends and young, have kept our show going for the past few years.

Ted and Patsy Miller, whose posts I took over, have a beautiful piece of land along the river. It will be pioneering for a few years, as there is nothing on it but the fencing.

Weather has been super this fall, with slight falls of snow that quickly disappear. It is so mild that the grass is showing signs of greening up again, but I hope we have snow for Christmas.

After toying with various invites for Christmas away from home, I have decided this year to stay put and cook my own turkey. The cabin is cozy and with the two cats, "Thomas" and "Bandit", along with "Dusty", my ten-year old pooch, it is hard to leave. "Thomas" is a six-month old sleek, black monster growing like a weed and learning wilderness ways from dear old Bandit, who is a survivor.

My eight-year old Siamese pal, "Smokey", succumbed to an owl or a coyote a year ago September 18th. I missed him sadly and tried in vain to find another. I think Thomas has some Siamese in him, being black and such a voice, which I am trying to stop with a spray gun, as he never stops, full or otherwise, but he is learning.

May God bless you all in the coming year.

Ye Olde Corby Cabin

Christmas 1990

How I wish you could all have seen the beauty of the Corby Place this morning (November 26th), a really authentic Christmas card, with a foot of glistening white snow, trees loaded, all sparkling with bright sunshine.

The horses are peacefully pawing away for their nourishment in the clearing, with the dark fir trees behind, a perfect setting.

"Thomas", my young black half-Siamese, comes with me wherever or whatever I am doing. Today, he inspected my roadwork as I cleared my two hills on the road. Highways would do it if I phoned, but I rather enjoy the work and I know they are dreadfully busy. The heaviest fall in 20 years here in the East Kootenay, I heard today.

This year, in October, saw the passing of my sister, Mary, the first break in my immediate family of my generation. My younger sister, Joan, her husband, Bud, and daughter, Susan, came from Ontario. It was good to see them, but the occasion, as always, sad.

For the past two days, I have been busy doing something I've wanted to do for years, updating my address and Christmas list. I found a large red exercise book that I hope will not get hidden under my various piles of what I can't part with! I am a collector and often wonder where it will all go.

My volunteer work includes Hospital Auxiliary, Library, and recycling bottles. The latter endeavor was sparked, and is run, by an energetic gal, Evelyn Barrington. We have made enough money, which is backed by government dollar for dollar, to beautify our local beach and to renovate our Community Hall. Also, plans are in the works for a tennis court and ice rink. So, with chores, wood and coal ashes, fencing repairs, etc., there is never a dull moment.

I cannot close this Christmas epistle without paying tribute to at least some of those whose kind thoughts and actions mean so much to me out here on the mountain. Water is such a very special treasure. No district water pipes here!

The water levels in the entire valley have been very low during the past few years, and my 160 acres are no exception. If by some mischance of forgetting that I can only run the water for so long, air gets in the pipe, and no water can be had! That is where friends come in, especially Herb Blakley. What a special blessing it is to see water in the tap again, after buckets and dippers!

Then there is the wood. Friends who hunt here surely help so much there. Others made metal "No Hunting" signs for me. Wooden ones, etc., simply get torn off or shot up! My wee fellowship from Canal Flats also is special in the wood needs of the Olde Corby Place. May the Lord richly bless them all.

It is cozy in the cabin now, as I write this at 10:30 p.m. Time to put my propane lights out and read in bed with my wee coal oil lamp.

God bless you all.

Christmas 1992

I find it hard to believe that this is nearly the end of November, Christmas only a month away, and no snow.

So much has happened here. Negotiations to part with a few acres for ostrich farming fell through, much to my relief. A new deal much more to my liking, which will leave the land as it is, untouched, is being processed. The outcome, hopefully, will provide me with a new small modern home with power, telephone, and all those goodies that at my stage in life all my friends say I should have.

Needless to say, I have thoroughly enjoyed the past 12 years in my wee log cabin, with all its necessary work, such as the woodpile, ashes, lamps, etc. It has been cozy and cool as the seasons went by. I only hope the new home will be as cozy. I certainly intend to have a wood-burner stove, regardless of new rules regarding pollution. I firmly believe wood smoke is harmless.

Water problems with my system gave my garden a bad time, until Herb Blakley finally thought it might just be in the line below the house to the barn and sure enough, it was.

The horses continue to be a great source of joy to me with their antics, often foreshadowing a change in the weather. They are very fortunate animals in my humble opinion, as they have a large area, 160 acres, in which to run and play.

It has been a joy lately, having longtime friends, Bob and Pat McGaw, from Vernon here. They come spring and fall on their journeys to visit their children. They help me tidy up around the cabin, splitting and piling wood. It looks so great to see it piled under the eaves. Friends from Windermere, who hunt through the place, also assist in so many ways, bringing wood and making me a cathouse.

What wonderful weather, mild, very little frost, with sunshine. Today, our first light snow that I don't think will stay.

May Our Lord richly bless you and yours.

Christmas 1993

Here I am, later than last year, November 29th, and still no letter written! So I must get cracking!

Fortunately, the recent cold snap has given up. It was 20° to 21°F below zero for five days. This morning was my first sleep-in as I didn't have to get up every six to seven hours to start the car! The car looks rather pretty. It is white with a red horse blanket on the hood. Sure helps to keep it warm.

As I said last year, I am waiting "patiently" for the government to okay a simple joining of two pieces of land. Folks in the know say it will be a year!! So, I am still looking forward to a modern house with power. I won't know myself, not having to worry about the car when it is safely plugged in!

Horses, as always, are a joy to me. I have seven so far, mostly ponies or small horses. One old-timer, "Nahanni", has been here for eight years. His owner is at the coast, and loves him dearly, but can't afford Lower Mainland boarding costs. The old fellow (19 years) had his teeth cared for this summer, but came from his summer grazing in rather poor condition so he is now on large amounts of good sweet feed, much to his joy. He is a gross eater, so that keeps the rest around hoping for some of the same. I only kept my Welsh mare, P.J., here this summer to let the grass come back and have her foal. She had a dandy filly born June 29th by the name of "Country Lady". I enjoyed caring for them when I should have been getting my knee looked after. Perhaps come spring I will get around to it.

"Corby", my problem dog, is still very disobedient when loose, likely the result of abuse before she came to me. I have the loan of a zapper; an expensive toy, but I can't use it because it is a remote control device that will have to wait until I have power, as the battery needs to be plugged in after use. However, she is a great joy in the house where she has two cats to contend with. "Thomas", five-year old part Siamese, enjoys "Corby's" rough play, but dear old fourteen-year old "Bandit" needs my watchful care. "Corby" is highly intelligent, but would love to get "Bandit" on the run! Needless to say, I have to keep "Corby" tied when not in the house. She would spend all day barking and bothering the horses.

I have missed seeing Bob and Pat McGaw this fall. This cold snap rather upset their plans. This is the earliest I can remember. A hunting friend kindly brought my coal from Calgary, just in time. I would have gone through a great deal of wood otherwise.

My wee log cabin is so easy to keep warm, but the cold snap reminded me of Prince George, when the radio kept us knowing the temperature all night!

Well, dears, must close with warm wishes to all, and may God richly bless you always.

Christmas 1994

How things are changing on the Olde Corby Place. My new house has the roof on and is looking just great. The start on the house was late due to many things, my trip to the Tegart Reunion in Ontario, August 13th and 14th, and my contractor friend, Kurt Hagen being unavailable. So I shall be in my cozy wee cabin until spring anyway, which is just fine as there are so many things to consider, such as flooring colours, carpet, etc.

My Open House New Year's Day, when I serve hot turkey sandwiches with homemade cranberry sauce, will be in the cabin for the last time. I started this in 1981. The cabin and I played host to many folk, coming and going. There were 16 folks in my 16' x14' cabin at one time, sitting on the floor or wherever.

All the animals, five horses, one cat, and one dog, are flourishing. "Bandit", I think, met his fate at age 14 years by either coyote or owl. He is greatly missed by "Thomas", or "Pusscat", as I call him. Now his affection for me shows in his great variety of meows, a different tone for all his wants. He is great company. Always waiting for me by the door.

I keep well, but still need to get my knee done when I am settled in the new home. Hopefully I will find the time.

The Tegart Reunion was great. I wouldn't have missed it for the world, especially seeing Corky and Nila and family, from Tucson, Arizona. Last was in 1973 on my Tegart tour. They were so wonderful to me.

My Christian friends in the family of God are so special. They fill my life in so many ways. My building contractor and bookkeeper, husband and wife, are dear Christians. Once a week I go to their home for supper and a session with the books. Pastor Bill Dorshuk, his family, and the whole congregation at Canal Flats are special. They come and cut wood, help with the irrigation ditch, and help with the maintenance on the car. May the Lord richly bless them always.

I can't close without telling you about my logging contractor, Don Dehart. Without his wonderful work and thought, my house would not be possible. Lloyd would have been so happy that the valuable timber had been so carefully harvested. One would never know that the place had been logged. Don is an environmental logger. What a blessing.

Friends from Devon, England, who now own my father's birthplace, enjoyed seeing the west with other friends, Herb and Peggy Blakley.

As usual, I am way behind on Christmas greetings, so please forgive. There are so many activities going on this month that I rarely eat dinner at home. Every evening seems to be booked.

So, with my love and God's blessing, I wish you all a very happy Christmas and all the best for the New Year.

Christmas 2000

Nancy, "Maxie", "Sylvester", and old "P.J." (15-year old Welsh mare) are all doing well. I am beginning to feel my 88 years, but am blessed with so many good friends who drop in for games of scrabble and to help me in various ways.

I am still boarding horses. At the moment, I have four horses and one mule. The mule is often the cause of much entertainment, when she gets them all running and bucking on their way to the buildings for water.

My nephew-partner, Peter Tegart, and his wife, Jarmilla, Alexandra (Ali) (26) and Danielle (20) at Ontario Western University are, though living and working in Vancouver, dearly loved and in contact often by phone. Peter was in London, England recently on business and was domiciled only a few doors from the Queen Mother. While there, he was able to see Winston Churchill's War Operations Room, just as it was during World War II. He brought back an illustrated pamphlet for me of Winston's war quarters during World War II.

The tremendous thought and work that Peter has put into this place gives me great comfort and peace of mind. The house is so comfortable and it has no stairs!

This summer, Peter and friend, Don Dehart, put in a really innovative irrigation system on the cleared acreage, which will make the place green, but I'm afraid will bring us mosquitoes! Having the beautiful spring water from the north end of the 160 acres on tap is a real luxury. This project entailed about a half mile of eight-foot underground piping, with a large storage tank near the spring. Don Dehart did these two water projects. Peter and Don worked hard in that hot, hot weather we had in August to put in the irrigation system, which will push irrigation water up electrically to a tank above the house. From there, it will be gravity flow. Peter, I know, is looking forward, as I am, to May when we will, hopefully, see it in operation. It is almost like being back at The Hidden Valley, only not doing the work!

My cozy house, with three heating systems (electric, propane, and wood) is, I'm afraid, always a constant muddle. I try to organize years of photos, memoranda, etc., as well as mail, letters to answer, etc. I still enjoy reading and have at least two books on the go. I haven't got time to get into mischief, if I was able!

Must say so long, aux wiedersein, etc. A very Happy Christmas to all and may God richly bless you.

Christmas 2002

It is with many wonderful memories that I will try to tell you some of them from this year. The Alberta girls led by my dear niece Sharon, who comes every August, had a weekend riding our mountain trails. How I wish I could be with them.

However, we did the next best thing. The got me up on "Dudley", Sharon's well trained paint. What a performance that was - a stool, the tailgate, and then "Dudley". Tracey took some excellent photos; one of them adorned a visitor's book and the cake at my birthday party.

What a do my 90th birthday party was on Saturday, September 28. We put it forward a month to humor the weather! Peter came up from Vancouver, a day's journey, on Wednesday the 25th. Jarmilla, his wife, and Danielle, his daughter, came for the weekend. Jarmilla teaches disabled children. Peter and Jarmilla welcomed their first grandchild, a little girl, to the family this year. Alexandra, "Ali" met her hubby Zarrell, a large seed grower from Indiana while guiding wealthy Americans around French Vineyards. Ali couldn't be at the party.

Susan Henley is my only niece from my side of the family. She was here for the party with her husband, Brian, and her four-year-old son, Tommy. They live in Surrey now, having recently moved from Ontario. It was so good to have a good chat with her. Sharon Wass, who is assisting me in my biography, made Susan's short visit a really enjoyable one because Sharon's son Dennis and Tommy really hit it off. Sharon took the boys bowling, Tommy's first time, while Susan, Brian, and I went to Strands.

Another wonderful surprise was John and Eileen Stevens from Crediton, England, my father's home village, came to my party. They had already been here in June. When Peter saw them he jokingly said, "Don't you folks ever go home?"

Don Dehart and Peter cleared the big shop. Everything went up into the loft or over to the old barn. The only thing left was my old cook stove that they used to display my cake. The Alberta girls had transformed the place using a harvest theme with corn leaves and stalks, bull rushes, and both fresh and dried arrangements. There were five round tables with chairs, inside and various seats available outside.

The local Legion ladies provided refreshments at 1P.M. when my nephew, Shiloh Tegart-a flying missionary, asked the blessing. It was so special seeing Shiloh again as he lives with his family in Riverton, Manitoba. He brought his mother, Heidi Tegart from Calgary with him.

My actual birthday weekend, Oct. 28th,had two parties; one with my cousin Dorothy and one with my dear friends Bill and Fay at Canal Flats. Dorothy was in Ireland for Sept. 28th so held a family get together at her house in Edgewater.

Sharon Wass took me over to Banff in October for a very special day. Quite unbeknownst to me she and her father, who lives and works in Banff, had arranged for me to be a celebrity!! Brewster CEO, Andrew Whittick, presented me with a fresh rose corsage and paid for our ride up Banff's famous Sulpher Mountain gondola and our lunch in the dining room where we could clearly see Lake Minnewanka in the distance. In the early fifties, long before there was a gondola, I had packed food and water with horses up Sulpher Mountain to the log restaurant at the top. The spring was half way up the mountain, but the food came from the hotel at the base. Back then the visitors all had to walk up and often slept on the trail, out in the open, to see the sunrise. It was a thrill to see the old trail with the 29 zigs and the 28 zags, slide by under the gondola.

Luckily this year we have had more rain and I now have three boarders belonging to friends. It is good to see them as the place has always had horses, ever since 1980 when I first moved into the wee log cabin. Up until recently, I have raised Welsh ponies as well as boarding other people's horses. Now the place is beautifully fenced with smooth wire under tension.

Until we meet again, may God bless you and keep you now and always.

Christmas 2003

It is with nostalgic memories of the Hidden Valley Ranch that I sit down to pen a few lines. I am here on the 160 acres of the Corby Place that Lloyd loved, where the Corby's and the Tegart's worked together when Lloyd and his brothers and sisters knew the place as well as their own home, the neighbouring Alpine Ranch.

We started out life together up north in Prince George, BC. Lloyd had a clearing contract with the P.G.E. (Pacific Great Eastern) on Please Go Easy! But every spring during break up, when roads in the bush were impassable, we always came back to the Olde Corby Place and lived in a tent. We would prune the fir trees for Christmas trees.

One morning we woke to a few inches of snow and two magnificent Bighorn Sheep rams standing on the side of the hill just above the tent. I now know that we are about at the southern edge of the Radium Hot Springs herd's range. Small herds (about five or six) often come through. I see them in the open area just above the house.

At this moment, Nov.8th, 5 pm., I am waiting for Helen Kipp, who is taking a card from me to Mavis Messerschmidt's 60th birthday "do" at Fairmont tonight. Mavis' home was my stopover place at night for many years. Before my road was pushed through I would be forced to stop over when the weather was too warm early spring or late fall as the access trail through the reserve was impassable until it froze early in the A.M. Many were the nights we sat up until 2 A.M. playing scrabble. Mavis helped celebrate the opening of my new grave road into the new place in 1985, which I finally got after much lobbying of Premier Bill Bennet's government by friends from England and the States. Even the Natives got involved as they did not want people going through the reserve, which was my only access.

Peter embarked on a new venture for the place. There was an experimental patch of Canola seed on ½ acre of the hay field. A group of scientists did everything except the irrigation, which we did. It was interesting to see the different varieties.

There was one row of male plants next to a row of female plants.

Peter is still busy with work, so I don't see him much. His daughter, Dani, was up this summer with some friends to go hiking. They wanted to hike up Mount Nelson. They went out despite the smoke from surrounding fires that wreathed the mountains. Now she is back at University in Ontario. Peter's granddaughter, Lily, is keeping everyone busy since she discovered the joy of opening drawers. She lives in Indiana with her parents. They are all going to Vancouver to spend Christmas with Peter and Jarmilla.

The place is looking well. Dell Wall looks after the ranch and my friend Elizabeth keeps my flower gardens looking lovely. We have been lucky to have plentiful water. Water is a concern everywhere on hot summers like this one. Fires devastated many parts of B.C. this summer. The Kootenay Park was closed most of the summer due to a large fire.

Brian Fiveland, who runs the Fairmont trial riding and camping, is boarding 16 horses here this winter. I love watching them come running down for water every day at noon.

Sharon Tegart arrived with some friends to help celebrate my 91st birthday. They bought a beautiful bunch of tulips and we all dined out. My friends Eleanor Statham and Ruby Nixon joined me at Vivien's for birthday lunch a couple of days later. They all kept me very busy.

My old home, the B Arrow ranch, is being developed into a subdivision called Castle Rock.

At the moment, late November, Elizabeth, my gardening friend, now that winter is here, is busy with her winter occupation of interior painting. She is painting my ceiling; it sure brightens up the place.

My cat, "Sylvester", has gone to be with Judy at Huxley, Alberta. I still have my old dog "Taffy".

So dears I must close with a heartfelt May God bless you.

Appendix 1

This information is from the research of Mr. Kerry York. Thanks to the "The Governors of the Schools of King Edward the Sixth, Birmingham."

THE CHRONICLE (School Magazine) March, 1927 (obituary)

It is with very great regret that we record the death, after a short illness of Mr. Lee, on December 12th 1926. Mr. Lee had been one of the French Masters since September 1917, and during that time he had gained the affection and respect of all with whom he came in contact. For some seven years he served in the OTC,[Officer's Training Corps] being in charge of signaling. He took an active interest in the games of the School, and was always ready to help in any way. He was assistant House Master of Heath's. Educated at Crediton Grammar School, he went to Christ's College Cambridge, and then lived in France and subsequently in Germany. He had been a master at Bowden College and came to us from Downside. His unfailing tact and kindly disposition both in and out of school will make his place hard to fill. We extend our deepest sympathy to Mrs. Lee.

BIRMINGHAM GAZETTE (local newspaper)
14th December, 1926: A Master's Death - Loss to King Edward's High School.

A sad ending to the term at King Edward's High School, New Street, Birmingham, was the death on Sunday, after a short illness, of Mr. Arnold Lee, of 40 Esme Road, Sparkhill, at the early age of 46. He had won a well-deserved place in the affections of all who knew him by his unassuming character, singular goodness of heart and self-effacement. Educated at Crediton Grammar School Mr. Lee went from there to Christ's College, Cambridge, taking his BA in 1902. Leaving Cambridge, he spent four years abroad, studying French and German, and before coming to King Edward's School in 1917, had been a master at Bowden College, Downside, and Cirencester Grammar School. For many years he held a commission in the Officers' Training Corps, and was well known on the school football [ie. rugby] and cricket ground. The sympathy of his many friends will go out to his widow and three children.

15th December, 1926: Funeral of Mr. A Lee

Most of the masters of King Edward's High School, New Street, Birmingham, attended the funeral of their late colleague Mr. Arnold Lee of 40 Esme Road Sparkhill, yesterday afternoon. There were also many scholars and old boys present at the service held at St John's Church, Sparkhill. The service was conducted by the Rev W Sneath*, assisted by the Vicar of Sparkhill the Rev Gordon Arrowsmith. The interment took
place at Yardley Wood Cemetery.

*Rev Sneath was a Mathematics Master at King Edward's School (1906-1935).

BIRMINGHAM POST & JOURNAL (local newspaper)
14th December, 1926: Mr. Arnold Lee

The end of term at King Edward's High School, Birmingham has been saddened by the death on Sunday, after a short illness of Mr. Arnold Lee of 40 Esme Road, Sparkhill, one of the masters, at the early age of 46. Mr. Lee's death is a serious loss to the school. He was not only valuable in the classroom, but took a large part in the general activities of the school, for many years holding a commission in the OTC, and was well-known on the school football and cricket ground, where his help was always readily given. He was himself a very useful athlete.

Appendix 2
The following article appeared in the Vernon Daily News and was reproduced in the Invermere Valley Echo, Thursday, October 2, 1975.

Nancy Tegart, Animal Babysitter

By Connie Metcalf

When a married couple with a family decide they need a holiday alone, they simply pay a babysitter, but what about couples who have not only children but horses, chickens or cattle?

Nancy Tegart, a widow who at one time alone managed the 760 acre ranch 20 miles northwest of Radium Hot Springs she and her late husband lived on for eight years, is in the unique business of caring for livestock when farmers decide they 'd like some time away from their chores.

"It has always been my desire to help people who have livestock to get away for a holiday because my husband and I went through this ourselves on the ranch; you're tied and the responsibility is very trying," said Nancy, a soft-spoken slight woman with a feeling for animals her current employers find remarkable.

"Nancy knows horses inside out and backwards," said Mrs. Barbara Edwards, of Valleycroft Farm off Brewer Road near Lavington, where Nancy has been looking after the Edward's three children, their seven horses, and chickens while Mrs. Edwards recovers from an operation.

"Nancy has diagnosed two horses ailments since she has been here," said Mrs. Edwards. "The first time she saw on of the horses eating, she knew it had a tooth problem."

Nancy and her purebred German Shepherd, Guard, her traveling companion, "lead a sort of wandering life together" traveling through B.C. and Alberta where Nancy says she seems to find friends and relatives "wherever I go."

"I may very well settle in this area, but I haven't decided yet," said Nancy, who is leaving Vernon this week for another job at Radium, and then plans a visit to Irricana, Alta., to see her niece and nephew, Sharon and Happy Tegart. Happy, the Canadian Bareback champion of 1968, has a Western Breeder artificial insemination operation which Nancy finds interesting and where she hopes to offer her assistance.

A woman who was raised on farms in B.C. and took over their huge ranch with more than 100 cattle when her husband, Lloyd, died develops a certain attachment to that way of life, and since Nancy gave up the ranch in 1971, she said she has always missed the livestock.

"Farming is in my blood," said Nancy, who finds her job as a traveling "nanny" for animals the perfect answer for her desire to be with them.

"I'm capable of handling small operations by myself or supervising larger ones," said Nancy, who can perform all tasks from animal midwife to ranch boss.

At a farm near Entwhistle, 60 miles west of Edmonton, Nancy pulled many calves last spring "when calving is a 24-hour job", as birth occurred during the night or when the farmer was busy doing something else.

One of Nancy's pet theories is the idea of putting Red Devon cattle, an English breed, on the Canadian range, as Nancy feels they are a good "middle of the road" breed which would adapt well to conditions here.

Although animals are her main occupation, Nancy has another interesting hobby of tracing down the history of her husband's family.

"There is only one family of Tegart's in North America," said Nancy, and her search to discover more about the family has taken her as far away as the Peace River Country, where she found her husband had a direct relative.

Keeping up with Nancy's travels is not an easy task, but for those in the Vernon or area farmers who feel they would like to know more about Nancy's "babysitting service" her permanent address is Box 100, Radium Hot Springs, B.C.

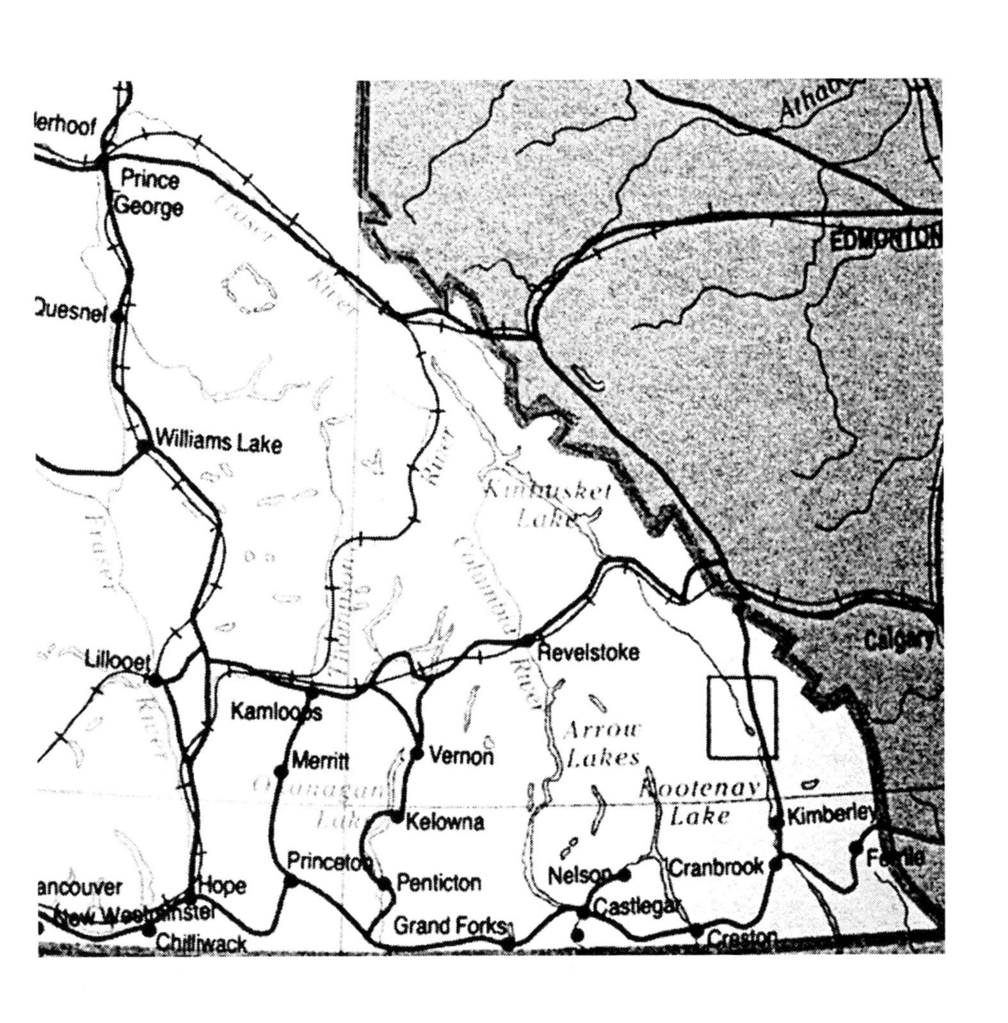

Prince
George
Quesnel
Williams Lake
Lillooet
Kamloops
Merritt
Vernon
Kelowna
Princeton
Penticton
Hope
New Westminster
Chilliwack
Grand Forks
Revelstoke
Arrow
Lakes
Lake
Nelson
Castlegar
Creston
Cranbrook
Kimberley
Calgary

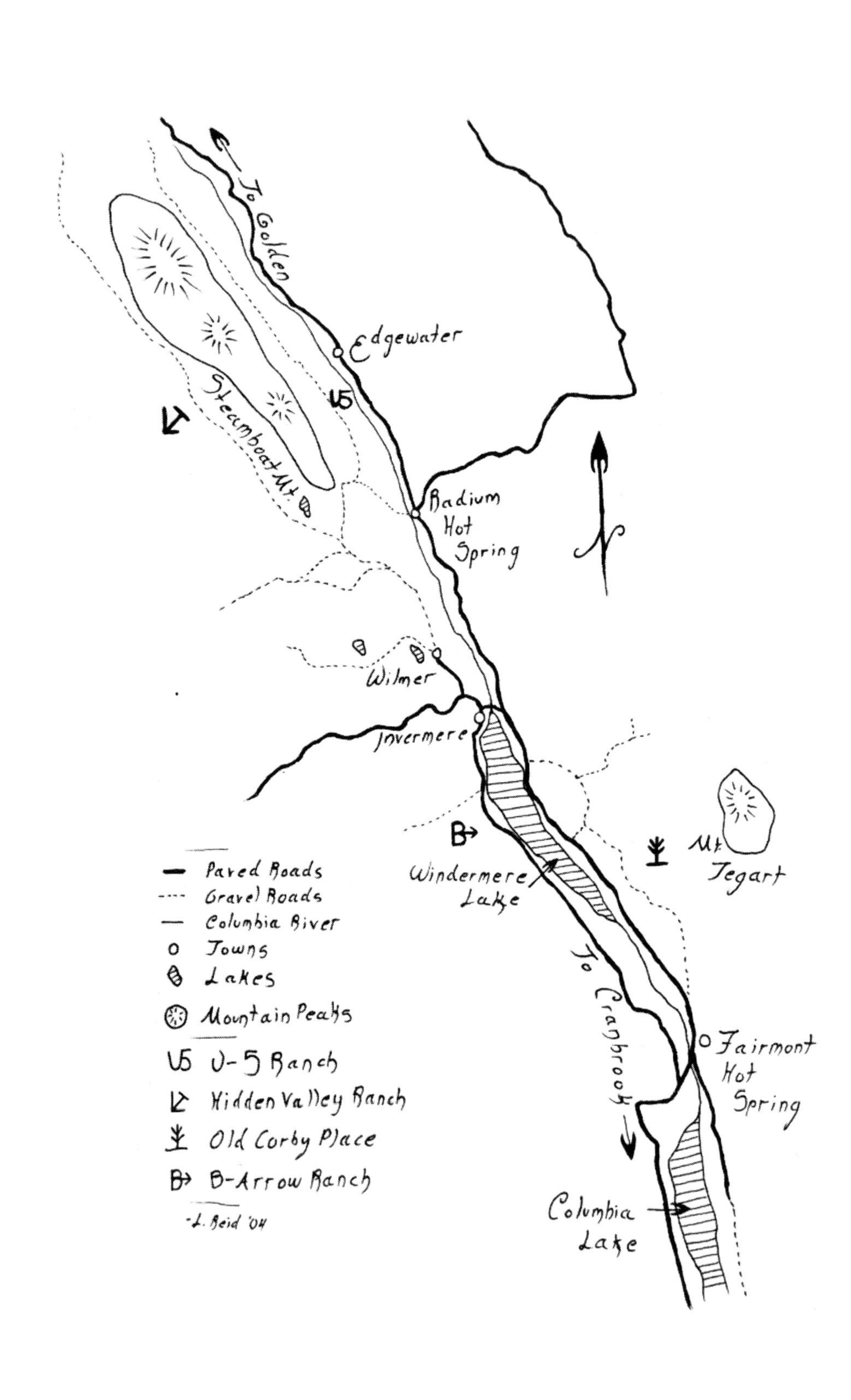
To Golden
Edgewater
Steamboat Mt.
Radium
Hot
Spring
Wilmer
Invermere
Windermere
Lake
Mt.
Tegart
To Cranbrook
Fairmont
Hot
Spring
Columbia
Lake
Paved Roads
Gravel Roads
Columbia River
Towns
Lakes
Mountain Peaks
U-5 Ranch
Hidden Valley Ranch
Old Corby Place
B-Arrow Ranch
-L. Reid '04

ISBN 141201861-7

9 781412 018616